KU-662-387

THE

MILLS & BOON®
Centenary Collection

**Celebrating 100 years of romance with
the very best of Mills & Boon**

First published in Great Britain 2008
by Harlequin Mills & Boon Limited,
Eton House, 18-24 Paradise Road, Richmond, Surrey TW9 1SR

© Betty Neels 2001

ISBN: 978 0 263 86617 9

77-0708

Harlequin Mills & Boon policy is to use papers that are
natural, renewable and recyclable products and made from
wood grown in sustainable forests. The logging and
manufacturing processes conform to the legal environmental
regulations of the country of origin.

Printed and bound in Spain
by Litografia Rosés S.A., Barcelona

The Doctor's Girl

by
Betty Neels

MILLS & BOON
Pure reading pleasure

Betty Neels spent her childhood and youth in Devonshire before training as a nurse and midwife. She was an army nursing sister during the war, married a Dutchman, and subsequently lived in Holland for fourteen years. Betty started to write on retirement from nursing, incited by a lady in a library bemoaning the lack of romantic novels. Betty Neels has sold over thirty-five million copies of her books worldwide.

Three of Betty's timeless classics appear in *Innocent Brides-To-Be* which is available in shops now, and don't miss her *Summer Engagements*, part of *The Queens of Romance* programme, which is out in August.

CHAPTER ONE

MISS MIMI CATTELL gave a low, dramatic moan followed by a few sobbing breaths, but when these had no effect upon the girl standing by the bed she sat up against her pillows, threw one of them at her and screeched, 'Well, don't just stand there, you little fool, phone Dr Gregg this instant. He must come and see me at once. I'm ill; I've hardly slept all night...' She paused to sneeze.

The girl by the bed, a small mousy person, very neat and with a rather plain face enlivened by a pair of vivid green eyes, picked up the pillow.

'Should you first of all try a hot lemon drink and some aspirin?' she suggested in a sensible voice. 'A cold in the head always makes one feel poorly. A day in bed, perhaps?'

The young woman in the bed had flung herself back onto her pillows again. 'Just do as I say for once. I don't pay you to make stupid suggestions. Get out and phone Dr Gregg; he's to come at once.' She moaned again. 'How can I possibly go to the Sinclairs' party this evening...?'

Dr Gregg's receptionist laughed down the phone.

'He's got three more private patients to see and then a clinic at the hospital, and it isn't Dr Gregg—he's gone off for a week's golf—it's his partner. I'll give him the message and you'd better say he'll come as soon as he can. She's not really ill, is she?'

'I don't think so. A nasty head cold…'

The receptionist laughed. 'I don't know why you stay with her.'

Loveday put down the phone. She wondered that too, quite often, but it was a case of beggars not being choosers, wasn't it? She had to have a roof over her head, she had to eat and she had to earn money so that she could save for a problematical future. And that meant another year or two working as Mimi Cattell's secretary—a misleading title if ever there was one, for she almost never sent letters, even when Loveday wrote them for her.

That didn't mean that Loveday had nothing to do. Her days were kept nicely busy—the care of Mimi's clothes took up a great deal of time, for what was the point of having a personal maid when Loveday had nothing else to do? Nothing except being at her beck and call each and every day, and if she came home later from a party at night as well.

Loveday, with only an elderly aunt living in a Dartmoor village whom she had never met, made the best of it. She was twenty-four, heartwhole and healthy, and perhaps one day a man would come along and sweep her off her feet. Common sense told her that this was unlikely to be the case, but a girl had to have her dreams…

She went back to the bedroom and found Mimi threshing about in her outsize bed, shouting at the unfortunate housemaid who had brought her break-fast tray.

Loveday prudently took the tray from the girl, who looked as if she was on the point of dropping it, nodded to her to slip away and said bracingly, 'The doctor will come as soon as he can. He has one or two patients to see first.' She made no mention of the clinic. 'If I fetch you a pot of China tea—weak with lemon—it may help you to feel well enough to have a bath and put on a fresh nightie before he comes.'

Mimi brightened. Her life was spent in making herself attractive to men, and perhaps she would feel strong enough to do her face. She said rudely, 'Get the tea, then, and make sure that the lemon's cut wafer-thin…'

Loveday went down to the basement, where Mrs Branch and the housemaid lived their lives. She took the tray with her and, being a practical girl, ate the fingers of toast on it and accepted the mug of tea Mrs Branch offered her. She should have had her breakfast with Mrs Branch and Ellie, but there wasn't much hope of getting it now. Getting Miss Cattell ready for the doctor would take quite a time. She ate the rest of the toast, sliced the lemon and bore a tray, daintily arranged, back upstairs.

Mimi Cattell, a spoilt beauty of society, prepared for the doctor's visit with the same care she took when getting ready for an evening party. 'And you can make the bed while I'm bathing—put some fresh pillowcases on, and don't dawdle…'

It was almost lunchtime by the time she was once more in her bed, carefully made up, wearing a gossamer nightgown, the fairytale effect rather marred by her sniffs. To blow her nose would make it red.

To Loveday's enquiry as to what she would like for lunch she said ill-temperedly that she had no appetite; she would eat something after he had visited her. 'And you'd better wait too; I want you here when he's examining me.'

'I'll fetch a jug of lemonade,' said Loveday, and sped down to the kitchen.

While Ellie obligingly squeezed lemons, she gobbled down soup and a roll; she was going to need all her patience, and the lowering feeling that the doctor might not come for hours was depressing.

She bore the lemonade back upstairs and presently took it down again; it wasn't sweet enough! She was kept occupied after that—opening the heavy curtains a little, then closing them again, longing to open a window and let a little London air into the room when Mimi sprayed herself once more with Chanel No 5. By now Mimi's temper, never long off the boil, was showing signs of erupting. 'He has no right to leave me in such distress,' she fumed. 'I need immediate attention. By the time he gets here I shall have probably got pneumonia. Find my smelling salts and give me the mirror from the dressing table.'

It was getting on for two o'clock when Loveday suggested that a little light lunch might make her employer feel better.

'Rubbish,' snarled Mimi. 'I won't eat a thing until he's examined me. I suppose you want a meal—well, you'll just have to wait.' Her high-pitched voice rose to a screech. 'I don't pay you to sit around and stuff yourself at my expense, you greedy little...'

The door opened by Ellie, and after one look the screech became a soft, patient voice. 'Doctor—at last...'

Mimi put up a hand to rearrange the cunning little curl over one ear to better advantage. 'I don't think we've met,' she purred. To Loveday, she said, 'Pull the curtains and get a chair for the doctor, and then go and stand by the window.' The commands were uttered in a very different voice.

The doctor opened the curtains before Loveday could get to them and pulled up a chair. 'I must introduce myself, Miss Cattell. I am Dr Gregg's partner and for the moment looking after his patients while he is away.'

Mimi said in a wispy voice, 'I thought you would never come. I am rather delicate, you know, and my health often gives cause for concern. My chest…'

She pushed back the bedspread and put a hand on her heart. It was annoying that he had turned away.

'Could we have the window open?' he asked Loveday.

A man after her own heart, thought Loveday, opening both windows despite Mimi's distressed cry. She would suffer for it later, but now a few lungfuls of London air would be heaven.

From where she stood she had a splendid view of the doctor. He was a tall man, with broad shoulders and fair hair flecked with grey. He was good-looking too, with a rather thin mouth and a splendid nose upon which were perched a pair of spectacles. A pity she couldn't see the colour of his eyes…

Miss Cattell's voice, sharp with impatience, brought her to the bedside. 'Are you deaf?' A remark hastily covered by a fit of sneezing, necessitating the use of a handkerchief and nose-blowing.

The doctor waited patiently until Mimi had resumed

her look of patient suffering. He said mildly, 'If you
will sit up, I'll listen to your chest.'

He had a deep voice, pleasantly impersonal, and he
appeared quite unimpressed by Mimi's charms,
ignoring her fluttering breaths and sighs, staring at the
wall behind the bed while he used his stethoscope.

'Clear as a bell,' he told her. 'A head cold. I suggest
aspirin, hot drinks and some brisk walks in the fresh
air—you are quite near Hyde Park, are you not? Eat
whatever you fancy and don't drink any alcohol.'

Mimi stared up at him. 'But I'm not well—I'm
delicate; I might catch a chill…'

'You have a head cold,' he told her gravely, and
Loveday had to admire his bedside manner. 'But you
are a healthy woman with a sound pair of lungs. You
will be perfectly fit in a couple of days—less, if you
do as I suggest.'

Mimi said rudely, 'I'll decide that for myself. When
will Dr Gregg be back? I don't know your name…?'

'Andrew Fforde.' He held out a large hand. 'I'm sure
you will let me know if you don't make a full recovery.'

Mimi didn't answer. Loveday went to the door with
him and said gravely, 'Thank you for coming, Doctor.'
She went downstairs with him, along the hall and
opened the front door. As he offered a hand and bade
her a grave good afternoon she was able to see that his
eyes were blue.

A sensible girl, she went first down to the kitchen,
where Mrs Branch and Ellie were sitting over a pot of
strong tea.

'I've saved you a bite of lunch,' said Mrs Branch,
and pushed a mug of tea across the table. 'That weren't
Dr Gregg. Ellie says 'e looked a bit of all right?'

'Dr Gregg's partner, and he was nice. Miss Cattell has a head cold.' Mrs Branch handed Loveday a cheese sandwich. 'You'll need that. Well, will she be going out this evening?'

'I should think so,' said Loveday in a cheese-thickened voice.

Miss Cattell was in a splendid rage; the doctor was a fool and she would speak to Dr Gregg about him the moment he was back. 'The man must be struck off,' declared Mimi. 'Does he realise that I am a private patient? And you standing there with the windows wide open, not caring if I live or die.'

Mimi tossed a few pillows around. 'Where have you been? You can get me a gin and tonic…'

'Doctor said no alcohol.'

'You'll do as I say! Make it a large one, and tell Cook to make me an omelette and a salad. I want it now. I shall rest and you can get everything ready for this evening.'

'You are going to the party, Miss Cattell?'

'Of course I am. I don't intend to disappoint my friends. I dare say I'll be home early. I'll ring for you if I am.'

Another half an hour went by while Mimi was rearranged in her bed, offered her omelette and given a second gin and tonic. She finally settled, the windows shut and curtains drawn, for a nap. Loveday, free at last, went to her room on the floor above, kicked off her shoes and got onto the bed. Some days were worse than others…

Miss Cattell was still asleep and snoring when Loveday crept into her room an hour later. In the kitchen once again, for yet another cup of tea, she thankfully accepted Mrs Branch's offer of a casserole kept hot in the oven for her supper. Mimi wouldn't leave the house before half past eight or nine o'clock, and there would be no chance to sit down to her supper before then.

Later, offering more China tea and wafer-thin bread and butter, Loveday was ordered to display a selection of the dresses Miss Cattell intended to wear. She meant to outshine everyone there and, her cold forgotten, she spent a long time deciding. After the lengthy ritual of bathing, making up her face and doing her hair, and finally being zipped into a flimsy dress which Loveday considered quite indecent, she changed her mind. The flimsy dress was thrown in a heap onto the floor and a striking scarlet outfit was decided upon, which meant that shoes and handbag had to be changed too—and while Loveday was doing that Ellie was ordered to bring another gin and tonic.

Loveday, escorting Mimi to a taxi, had the nasty feeling that the night was going to prove worse than the day had been. She was right; she was wakened at two in the morning by the noisy return of Miss Cattell and several of her friends, who thankfully didn't stay, but that meant she had to go downstairs and help Mimi up to her room.

This was no easy task; Mimi was too drunk to help herself, so that hoisting her upstairs and into her room was a herculean task. Loveday was strong even though she was small, but by the time she had rolled the lady onto her bed she decided that enough was enough. She removed Mimi's shoes, covered her with a light blanket and went back to her own bed.

In a few hours she had to get up again and face Miss

Cattell's rage at discovering herself still clad in scarlet crêpe, lying untidily under a blanket. Even worse than that, her dress was torn and stained; Loveday had never heard such language…

When Miss Cattell was once more bathed, her make-up removed, and attired in a satin and lace confection, she declared that she would remain in bed for the rest of the day. 'My cold is still very heavy.' She snorted. 'Cold indeed. That man had no idea of what he was talking about.'

Loveday allowed her thoughts to dwell upon him, and not for the first time. She had liked him. If she were ever ill she would like him to look after her. She frowned. In different surroundings, of course, and in a nightie like Miss Cattell wore. She dismissed the thought as absurd, but as the day wore on it was somehow restful to think about him while Mimi's cross voice went on and on.

On her half-day off, she went to the public library and searched the papers and magazines, looking for jobs. 'Computer skills…knowledge of a foreign language useful…anyone under the age of twenty-five need not apply…kitchen hands willing to work late nights…' A splendid selection, but none of them would do. And they all ended with references required. She didn't think that Miss Cattell would give her a reference, not one which would secure her a job.

As it turned out she was quite right.

It was Mrs Branch who told her that Miss Cattell had quarrelled with the man she had decided she would marry, which was possibly an excuse for her to be even more bad-tempered than usual, and solace herself by filling the house with her friends, going on a shopping spree and staying up until all hours.

It was on the morning after one of Mimi's parties that a bouquet of roses was delivered. They must be arranged at once, she ordered, and there was a particularly lovely vase into which they must go.

Loveday arranged them carefully under her employer's eye and bore them from room to room while Mimi decided where they should go. It was unfortunate that, getting impatient, she turned sharply and knocked the vase and flowers out of Loveday's hands.

'My vase,' she screamed. 'It was worth hundreds of pounds. You careless fool; you'll pay for this...' She gave Loveday a whack over one eye. 'You're fired. Get out now before I send for the police!'

'If anyone sends for the police it will be myself,' said Loveday. 'It was your fault that I dropped the vase and you hit me. I shall leave at once and you can do what you like.' She added, 'I'm very glad to be going.'

Miss Cattell went an ugly red. 'You'll not get a reference from me.'

'I don't expect one. Just a week's wages in lieu of notice.'

Loveday left Mimi standing there and went to her room and packed her few things tidily before going down to the kitchen.

'I'm leaving,' she told Mrs Branch. 'I shall miss you and Ellie; you've both been very kind to me.'

'You're going to have a black eye,' said Mrs Branch. 'Sit down for a second and drink a cup of tea. Where will you go?'

'I don't know...'

'Well, if it's any help, I've a sister who lives near Victoria Park—Spring Blossom Road—she has rooms.

Wait a tick while I write 'er a line. She'll put you up while you sort yerself out.'

Ellie hadn't said a word, but she cut ham sandwiches and wrapped them neatly and gave them to Loveday. It was a kind gesture which almost melted Loveday's icy calm.

She left the house shortly afterwards; she had her week's wages as well as what was owed her in her purse, but she tried not to think of the things Mimi had said to her. It would have been a pleasure to have torn up the money and thrown it at her, but she was going to need every penny of it.

Mrs Branch's sister, Mrs Slade, lived a far cry from Miss Cattell's fashionable house. Loveday, with Mrs Branch's directions written on the back of an envelope, made her way there, lugging her case and shoulder bag. It was a long journey, but there was a lull in the traffic before the lunch hour and the bus queues were short.

Spring Blossom Road couldn't have seen a spring blossom for many years; it was a short, dingy street with small brick houses on either side of it. But it was tolerably quiet and most of the windows had cheerful curtains. It was a relief to find that Mrs Slade had the same kind, cheerful face as her sister. She read Mrs Branch's note and bade Loveday go in.

"Appens I've got the basement vacant,' she told Loveday. 'It's a bit dark, but it's clean.' She smiled suddenly. 'Not what you've been used to, from what I've 'eard. Take it for a week while you find yourself a job. It'll be rent in advance but I'll not overcharge you.'

Then she led the way to the back of the house, told Loveday to sit down at the kitchen table and offered tea.

'That's a nasty eye you've got there—Miss Cattell had one of her tantrums? My sister only stays until Ellie gets married. I don't 'old with these idle folk with nothing better to do than get nasty.'

The tea was hot and strong and sweet and Loveday felt better. This was something which had been bound to happen sooner or later; she should count herself lucky that Mrs Branch had been so kind and helpful and that she had two weeks' wages in her bag.

She went with Mrs Slade to inspect the basement presently. It was a small room below street level, so that the only view was of feet passing the window. But there was a divan bed, a table, two chairs and a shabby armchair by a small electric fire. There was a sink in one corner, and a small door which led to the neglected strip of back garden. 'Outside lav. Nice and handy for you,' explained Mrs Slade. "Ere's a key, and you'd better pop down to the corner and get yourself some food. There is a gas ring by the sink so you can cook if you want to.'

So Loveday went to the small shops at the end of the road and bought eggs, butter, tea and a bottle of milk. She still had the ham sandwiches, which would do very nicely for her supper...

She was a sensible girl, and now that her boats were burnt behind her she was cheerfully optimistic. Loveday ate her sandwiches, drank more tea and contrived to wash at the sink before venturing cautiously into the back garden to find the loo. And then, tired by such an eventful day, she got onto the divan and went to sleep. Her eye was painful but there was no mirror for her to inspect it, only her tiny powder compact which was quite inadequate.

It was raining in the morning and there was the first chill of autumn in the air. Loveday boiled an egg, counted her money and sat down to plan her day. She couldn't remember her mother and father, who had both died in a rail crash while she was still a toddler, but the stern aunt who had brought her up had instilled in her a number of useful adages. 'Strike while the iron is hot' was one of them, and Loveday intended to do just that.

She would visit the nearest job centre, the public library, and make a round of the adverts in the small shop windows. That would be a start. But before she did, she allowed her thoughts to wander a little. Miss Cattell would certainly insist on Dr Gregg visiting her, and if she did that she would be able to complain about Dr Fforde. She hoped she would not; they hadn't exchanged two words and yet she had the firm feeling that she knew him well.

Her eye was painful and almost closed, and, had she but known it, was the reason why the job centre lady wasn't very helpful. She had to admit that it looked rather awful when she caught sight of it in a passing shop window. Tomorrow, if it wasn't better, she would go to the nearest hospital and get something for it. Next she applied for a job as a waitress in a large, noisy café and was told to stop wasting time by the proprietor.

'Oo's going to order from a girl with an eye like that? Been in a fight, 'ave yer?'

The next morning she caught a bus to the hospital, a mile away. It was a vast Victorian building, its Casualty already overflowing. Since Loveday's eye wasn't an urgent case, she was told to sit on one of the crowded benches and wait.

The benches didn't seem any less crowded; rather the opposite. At midday she got a cup of coffee and a roll from the canteen and then settled down to wait again. She was still waiting when Fforde, on his way to take a clinic in outpatients, took a short cut there through Casualty. He was late and he hardly noticed the sea of faces looking hopefully at him. He was almost by the end doors when he caught sight of Loveday, or rather he caught sight of the black eye, now a rainbow of colours and swollen shut.

It was the mouse-like girl who had been with that abominable Miss Cattell. Why was she here in the East end of London with an eye like that? He had felt an instant and quite unexpected liking for her when he had seen her, and now he realised that he was glad to have found her again, even if the circumstances were peculiar. He must find out about her… He was through the doors by now and encircled by his clerk, his houseman and Sister, already touchy because he was late.

Of course by the time he had finished his clinic the Casualty benches were almost empty and there was no sign of her. Impelled by some feeling he didn't examine, he went to Casualty and asked to see the cases for the day. 'A young lady with a black eye,' he told the receptionist. 'Have you her address? She is concerned with one of my patients.'

The receptionist was helpful; she liked him, for he was polite and friendly and good-looking. 'Miss Loveday West, unemployed, gave an address in Spring Blossom Road. That's turn left from here and half a mile down the road. Had her eye treated; no need to return.'

He thanked her nicely, then got into his car and drove back to his consulting room. He had two patients to see and he was already late…

There was no reason why he should feel this urge to see her again; he had smiled briefly, they had exchanged goodbyes on the doorstep and that was all. But if the opportunity should occur…

Which it did, and far more rapidly than he anticipated.

Waiting for him when he reached his rooms on the following morning was Miss Priss, his receptionist-secretary. She was a thin lady of middle years, with a wispy voice and a tendency to crack her knuckles when agitated, but nevertheless she was his mainstay and prop. Even in her agitation she remembered to wish him a good morning before explaining that she had had bad news; she needed to go home at once—her mother had been taken ill and there was no one else…

Dr Fforde waited until she had drawn breath. 'Of course you must go at once. Take a taxi and stay as long as you wish to. Dr Gregg will be back today, and I'm not busy. We shall manage very well. Have you sufficient money? Is there anyone you wish to telephone?'

'Yes, thank you, and there is nobody to phone.'

'Then get a taxi and I'll ask Mrs Betts to bring you a cup of tea.'

Mrs Betts, who kept the various consulting rooms clean, was like a sparrow, small and perky and pleased to take a small part in any dramatic event.

Miss Priss, fortified by what Mrs Betts called her 'special brew', was seen on her way, and then Dr Fforde sat down at his desk and phoned the first agency in the phone book. Someone would come, but not until the afternoon. It was fortunate that Mr Jackson, in the rooms above him, was away for the day and his secretary agreed to take Miss Priss's place for the morning...

The girl from the agency was young, pretty and inefficient. By the end of the next day Dr Fforde, a man with a well-controlled temper, was having difficulty in holding it in check. He let himself into his small mews house, tucked away behind a terrace of grand Georgian mansions, and went from the narrow hall into the kitchen, where his housekeeper, Mrs Duckett, was standing at the table making pastry.

She took a look at his tired face. 'A nice cuppa is what you're needing, sir. Just you go along to your study and I'll bring it in two shakes of a lamb's tail. Have you had a busy day?'

He told her about Miss Priss. 'Then you'll have to find someone as good as her to take her pace,' said Mrs Duckett.

He went to his study, lifted Mrs Duckett's elderly cat off his chair and sat down with her on his knee. He had letters to write, a mass of paperwork, patients' notes to read, and the outline of a lecture he was to give during the following week to prepare. He loved his work, and with Miss Priss to see to his consulting room and remind him of his daily appointments he enjoyed it. But not, he thought savagely, if he had to endure her replacement—the thought of another day of her silly giggle and lack of common sense wouldn't bear contemplating.

Something had to be done, and even while he thought that he knew the answer.

Loveday had gone back from the hospital knowing that it wasn't much use looking for work until her eye looked more normal. It would take a few days, the casualty officer had told her, but her eye hadn't been damaged. She should bathe it frequently and come back if it didn't improve within a day or so.

So she had gone back to the basement room with a tin of beans for lunch and the local paper someone had left on the bench beside her. It was a bit late for lunch, so she'd had an early tea with the beans and gone to bed.

A persistent faint mewing had woken her during the small hours, and when she'd opened the door into the garden a very small, thin cat had slunk in, to crouch in a corner. Loveday had shut the door, offered milk, and watched the small creature gulp it down, so she'd crumbled bread into more milk and watched that disappear too. It was a miserable specimen of a cat, with bedraggled fur and bones and it had been terrified. She'd got back into bed, and presently the little beast had crept onto the old quilt and gone to sleep.

'So now I've got a cat,' Loveday had said, and went off to sleep too.

This morning her eye was better. It was still hideously discoloured but at least she could open it a little. She dressed while she talked soothingly to the cat and presently, leaving it once more crouching there in the corner, she went to ask Mrs Slade if she knew if it belonged to anybody.

'Bless you, no, my dear. People who had it went away and left it behind.'

'Then would you mind very much if I had it? When I find work and perhaps have to leave here, I could take it with me.'

'And why not? No one else will be bothered with the little creature. Yer eye is better.'

'I went to the hospital. They said it would be fine in another day or two.'

Mrs Slade looked her up and down. 'Got enough to eat?'

'Oh, yes,' said Loveday. 'I'm just going to the shops now.'

She bought milk and bread and more beans, and a tin of rice pudding because the cat so obviously needed nourishing, plus cat food and a bag of apples going cheap. Several people stopped to say what a nasty eye she had.

She and the cat had bread and butter and milk pudding for lunch, and the cat perked up enough to make feeble attempts to wash while Loveday counted her money and did sums. The pair of them got into the chair presently and dozed until it was time to boil the kettle and make tea while the cat had the last of the rice pudding.

It was bordering on twilight when there was a thump on the door. The cat got under the divan and after a moment there was another urgent thump on the door. Loveday went to open it.

'Hello,' said Dr Fforde. 'May I come in?'

He didn't wait for her to close her astonished mouth but came in and shut the door. He said pleasantly, 'That's a nasty eye.'

There was no point in pretending she didn't know who he was. Full of pleasure at the sight of him, and imbued with the feeling that it was perfectly natural for him to come and see her, she smiled widely.

'How did you know where I was?'

'I saw you at the hospital. I've come to ask a favour of you.'

'Me? A favour?' She glanced round her. 'But I'm hardly in a position to grant a favour.'

'May we sit down?' And when she was in the armchair he sat carefully on the old kitchen chair opposite. 'But first, may I ask why you are here? You were with Miss Cattell, were you not?'

'Well, yes, but I dropped a vase, a very expensive one...'

'So she slapped you and sent you packing?'

'Yes.'

'So why are you here?'

'Mrs Branch, she is Miss Cattell's cook, sent me here because Mrs Slade who owns it is her sister and I had nowhere to go.'

The doctor took off his specs, polished them, and put them back on. He observed pleasantly, 'There's a cat under the bed.'

'Yes, I know. He's starving. I'm going to look after him.'

The doctor sighed silently. Not only was he about to take on a mousy girl with a black eye but a stray cat too. He must be mad!

'The favour I wish to ask of you: my receptionist at my consulting rooms has had to return home at a moment's notice; would you consider taking her place until she returns? It isn't a difficult job—opening the post, answering the phone, dealing with patients. The hours are sometimes odd, but it is largely a matter of common sense.'

Loveday sat and looked at him. Finally, since he was sitting there calmly waiting for her to speak, she said, 'I can type and do shorthand, but I don't understand computers. I don't think it would do because of my eye—and I can't leave the cat.'

'I don't want you to bother with computers, but typing would be a bonus, and you have a nice quiet voice and an unobtrusive manner—both things which patients expect and do appreciate. As for the cat, I see no reason why you shouldn't keep it.'

'Isn't it a long way from here to where you work? I do wonder why you have come here. I mean, there must be any number of suitable receptionists from all those agencies.'

'Since Miss Priss went two days ago I have endured the services of a charming young lady who calls my patients "dear" and burst into tears because she broke her nail on the typewriter. She is also distractingly pretty, which is hardly an asset for a job such as I'm offering you. I do not wish to be distracted, and my patients have other things on their minds besides pretty faces.'

Which meant, when all was said and done, that Loveday had the kind of face no one would look at twice. Background material, that's me, thought Loveday.

'And where will I live?'

'There is a very small flat on the top floor of the house where I have my rooms. There are two other medical men there, and of course the place is empty at night. You could live there—and the cat, if you wish.'

'You really mean that?'

All at once he looked forbidding. 'I endeavour to say what I mean, Miss West.'

She made haste to apologise. 'What I really mean is that you don't know anything about me and I don't know anything about you. We're strangers, aren't we? And yet here you are, offering me a job,' she added hastily, in case he had second thoughts. 'It sounds too good to be true.'

'Nevertheless, it is a genuine offer of work—and do not forget that only the urgency of my need for adequate help has prompted me to offer you the job. You are at liberty to leave if you should wish to do so, providing you give me adequate time to find a replacement. If Miss Priss should return she would, of course, resume her work; that is a risk for you.' He smiled suddenly. 'We are both taking a risk, but it is to our advantage that we should help each other.'

Such terms of practicability and common sense made the vague doubts at the back of Loveday's head melt away. She had had no future, and now all at once security—even if temporary—was being handed her on a plate.

'All right,' said Loveday. 'I'll come.'

'Thank you. Could you be ready if I fetch you at half past eight tomorrow morning? My first patient is at eleven-thirty, which will give you time to find your way around.'

He stood up and held out a hand. 'I think we shall deal well with each other, Miss West.'

She put her hand in his and felt the reassuring firmness of it.

'I'll be ready—and the cat. You haven't forgotten the cat?'

'No, I haven't forgotten.'

CHAPTER TWO

LOVEDAY went to see Mrs Slade then, and in answer to that lady's doubtful reception of her news assured her that Dr Fforde was no stranger.

'Well, yer a sensible girl, but if you need an 'elping 'and yer know where to come.'

Loveday thanked her. 'I'll write to you,' she said, 'and I'll write to Mrs Branch too. I think it's a job I can manage, and it will be nice to have somewhere to live where I can have the cat.'

She said goodbye and went back to the basement, and, since a celebration was called for, she gave the cat half the cat meat and boiled two eggs.

In the morning she was a bit worried that the cat might try and escape, but the little beast was still too weak and weary to do more than cling to her when the doctor arrived. His good morning was businesslike as he popped her into the car, put her case into the boot and got in and drove away.

He was still glad to see her, but he had a busy day ahead of him and a day was only so long...

Loveday, sensing that, made no effort to talk, but sat

clutching the cat, savouring the delight of being driven in a Bentley motor car.

His rooms were in a house in a quiet street, one in a terrace of similar houses. He ushered her into the narrow hall with its lofty ceiling and up the handsome staircase at its end. There were several doors on the landing, and as they started up the next flight he nodded to the end one.

'I'm in the end room. We'll go to your place first.'

They went up another flight of stairs past more doors and finally up a small staircase with a door at the top.

The doctor took a key from a pocket and opened it. It gave directly into a small room, its window opening onto the flat roof of the room below. There were two doors but he didn't open them.

'The porter will bring up your case. And I asked him to stock up your cupboard. I suggest you feed the cat and leave the window shut and then come down to my room. Ten minutes?'

He had gone, leaving her to revolve slowly, trying to take it all in. But not for long. Ten minutes didn't give her much time. She opened one of the doors and found a small room with just space for a narrow bed, a table, a mirror and a chair. It had a small window and the curtains were pretty. Still with the cat tucked under her arm, she opened the other door. It was a minute kitchen, and between it and the bedroom was an even smaller shower room.

Loveday sucked in her breath like a happy child and went to the door to see who was there. It was the porter with her case.

'Todd's the name, miss. I'm here all day until seven o'clock, so do ask if you need anything. Dr Fforde said you've got a cat. I'll bring up a tray and suchlike before

I go. There's enough in the cupboard to keep you going for a bit.'

She thanked him, settled the cat on the bed and offered it food, then tidied her hair, powdered her nose and went down to the first floor, the door key in her pocket. She should have been feeling nervous, but there hadn't been time.

She knocked and walked in. This was the waiting room, she supposed, all restful greys and blues, and with one or two charming flower paintings on the walls. There was a desk in one corner with a filing cabinet beside it.

'In here,' said Dr Fforde, and she went through a half-open door to the room beyond where he sat at his desk. He got up as she went in.

He noticed with satisfaction that she looked very composed, as neat as a new pin, and the black eye was better, allowing for a glint of vivid green under the lid.

'I'll take you round and show you where everything is, and we will have coffee while I explain your work. There should be time after that for you to go around on your own, just to check things. As I told you, there are few skills required—only a smiling face for all the patients and the ability to cope with simple routine.'

He showed her the treatment room leading from his consulting room. 'Nurse Paget comes about ten o'clock, unless I've a patient before then. She isn't here every day, so she will explain her hours to you when you meet her. Now, this is the waiting room, which is our domain.'

Her duties were simple. Even at such short notice she thought that she would manage well enough, and there would be no one there in the afternoon so she

would have time to go over her duties again. There
would be three patients after five o'clock, he told her.

'Now, your hours of work. You have an early-
morning start—eight o'clock—an hour for lunch,
between twelve and one, and tea when you have half an
hour to spare during the afternoon. You'll be free to
leave at five o'clock, but I must warn you that frequently
I have an evening patient and you would need to be here.
You have half-day on Saturday and all Sunday free, but
Miss Priss came in on Saturday mornings to get everything ready for Monday. Can you cope with that?'

'Yes,' said Loveday. 'You will tell me if I don't do
everything as you like it?'

'Yes. Now, salary…' He mentioned a sum which
made her blink the good eye.

'Too much,' said Loveday roundly. 'I'm living rent-
free, remember.'

She encountered an icy blue stare. 'Allow me to
make my own decisions, Miss West.'

She nodded meekly and said, 'Yes, Doctor,' but there
was nothing meek about the sparkle in her eye. She
would have liked to ask him to stop calling her Miss
West with every breath, but since she was in his employ
she supposed that she would have to answer to anything
she felt he wished to call her.

That night, lying in her bed with the cat wrapped in
one of her woolies curled up at her feet, Loveday, half
asleep, went over the day. The two morning patients
had been no problem; she had greeted them by name
and ushered them in and out again, dealt with their appointments and filed away their notes and when the
doctor, with a brief nod, had gone away, she had locked
the door and come upstairs to her new home.

Todd had left everything necessary for the cat's comfort outside the door. She had opened the window onto the flat roof, arranged everything to her satisfaction and watched the cat creep cautiously through the half-open window and then back again. She'd fed him then, and made herself a cheese sandwich and a cup of coffee from the stock of food neatly stacked away in the kitchen.

The afternoon she had spent prowling round the consulting rooms, checking and re-checking; for such a magnificent wage she intended to be perfect...

The doctor had returned shortly before the first of his late patients, refused the tea she had offered to make him, and when the last one had gone he'd gone too, observing quietly that she appeared to have settled in nicely and bidding her goodnight. She had felt hurt that he hadn't said more than that, but had consoled herself with the thought that he led a busy life and although he had given her a job and a roof over her head that was no reason why he should concern himself further.

She had spent a blissful evening doing sums and making a list of all the things she would like to buy. It was a lengthy list...

Dr Fforde had taken himself off home. There was no doubt about it, Loveday had taken to her new job like a duck to water. His patients, accustomed to Miss Priss's austere politeness, had been made aware of the reason for her absence, and had expressed polite concern and commented on the suitability of her substitute. She might not have Miss Priss's presence but she had a pleasant manner and a quiet voice which didn't encroach...

He'd had an urgent call from the hospital within ten minutes of his return to his home. His work had taken over then, and for the time being, at least, he had forgotten her.

Loveday slept soundly with the cat curled up on her feet, and woke with the pleasant feeling that she was going to enjoy her day. She left the cat to potter onto the roof, which it did, while she showered and dressed and got breakfast. She wondered who had had the thoughtfulness to get several tins of cat food as she watched the little beast scoff its meal.

'You're beginning to look like a cat,' she told him, 'and worthy of a name.' When he paused to look at her, she added, 'I shall call you Sam, and I must say that it is nice to have someone to talk to.'

She made him comfortable on the woolly, left the window open and went down to the consulting room.

It was still early, and there was no one about except the porter, who wished her a cheerful good morning. 'Put your rubbish out on a Friday,' he warned her. 'And will you be wanting milk?'

'Yes, please. Does the milkman call?'

'He does. I'll get him to leave an extra pint and I'll put it outside your door.'

She thanked him and unlocked the waiting room door. For such a magnificent sum the doctor deserved the very best attention; she dusted and polished, saw to the flowers in their vases, arranged the post just so on his desk, got out the patients' notes for the day and put everything ready to make coffee. That done, she went and sat by the open window and watched the quiet street below. When the Bentley whispered to a halt below she went and sat down behind her desk in the corner of the room.

The doctor, coming in presently, glanced at her as he wished her a brisk good morning and sighed with silent relief. She hadn't been putting on a show yesterday; she really was composed and capable, sitting there sedately, ready to melt into the background until she was wanted.

He paused at his door. 'Any problems? You are quite comfortable upstairs?'

'Yes, thank you, and there are no problems. Would you like coffee? It'll only take a minute.'

'Please. Would you bring it in?'

Since she made no effort to attract attention to herself he forgot her, absorbed in his patients, but remembered as he left to visit those who were housebound or too ill to come and see him, to wish her good morning and advise her that he would be back during the afternoon.

Loveday, eating her lunchtime sandwich, leaning out of the window watching Sam stretched out in the autumn sunshine, told the cat about the morning's work, the patients who had come, and the few bad moments she had had when she had mislaid some notes.

'I found them, luckily,' she explained to him. 'I can't afford to slip up, can I, Sam? I don't wish Miss Priss to be too worried about her mother, but I do hope she won't come back until I've saved some money and found a job where you'll be welcome.'

Sam paused in his wash and brush-up and gave her a look. He was going to be a handsome cat, but he wasn't young any more, so a settled life would suit him down to the ground. He conveyed his feelings with a look, and Loveday said, 'Yes, I know, Sam. But I'll not part with you, I promise.'

At the end of the week she found an envelope with her wages on her desk, and when she thanked the doctor he said, 'I'll be away for the weekend. You'll be here in the morning? Take any phone calls, and for anything urgent you can reach me at the number on my desk. Set the answering-machine when you leave. I have a patient at half past nine on Monday morning.' At the door he paused. 'I hope you have a pleasant weekend.'

At noon on Saturday she locked the consulting rooms and went to her little flat. With Sam on her lap she made a shopping list, ate her lunch and, bidding him to be a good boy, set off to the nearest shops. The porter had told her that five minutes' walk away there were shops which should supply her needs. 'Nothing posh,' he said. 'Been there for years, they have, very handy, too.'

She soon found them, tucked away behind the rather grand houses: the butcher, the baker, the greengrocer, all inhabiting small and rather shabby shops, but selling everything she had on her list. There was a newsagent too, selling soft drinks, chocolates and sweets, and with a shelf of second-hand books going cheap.

Loveday went back to her flat and unpacked her carrier bags. She still wasn't sure when she could get out during the day, and had prudently stocked up with enough food to last for several days. That done, she sat down to her tea and made another list—clothes, this time. They were a pipe dream at the moment, but there was no harm in considering what she would buy once she had saved up enough money to spend some of it.

It was very quiet in the house. Todd had locked up and gone home, and the place would be empty now until he came again around six o'clock on Monday morning. Loveday wasn't nervous; indeed she welcomed the silence after Miss Cattell's voice raised unendingly in demands and complaints. She washed her hair and went to bed early, with Sam for company.

She went walking on Sunday, to St James's Park and then Hyde Park, stopping for coffee on the way. It was a chilly day but she was happy. To be free, with money in her purse and a home to go back to—what more could she ask of life? she reflected. Well, quite a bit, she conceded—a husband, children and a home... and to be loved.

'A waste of time,' said Loveday, with no one to hear her. 'Who would want to marry me in the first place and how would I ever meet him?'

She walked on briskly. He would have to love her even though she wasn't pretty, and preferably have enough money to have a nice home and like children. Never mind what he looked like... She paused. Yes, she did mind—he would need to be tall and reassuringly large, and she wouldn't object to him wearing specs on his handsome nose...

'You're being ridiculous,' said Loveday. 'Just because he's the only man who has spoken to you for years.'

She took herself off back home and had a leisurely lunch—a lamb chop, sprouts and a jacket potato, with a tub of yoghurt for pudding—and then sat in the little armchair with Sam on her lap and read the Sunday paper from front to back. And then tea, and later supper and bed.

'Some would call it a dull day, but we've enjoyed every minute of it,' she told Sam.

The week began well. The nurse, whom she seldom saw, had treated her with coolness at first, and then, realising that Loveday presented no risk to her status, became casually friendly. As for Dr Fforde, he treated her with the brisk, friendly manner which she found daunting. But such treatment was only to be expected….

It was almost the end of the week when he came earlier than usual to the consulting rooms. She gave him coffee and, since she was for the moment idle, paused to tell him that Sam had turned into a handsome cat. 'And he's very intelligent,' she added chattily. 'You really should come up and see him some time…'

The moment she had uttered them she wished the words unsaid. The doctor's cool, 'I'm glad to hear that he has made such a good recovery,' uttered in a dismissive voice sent the colour into her cheeks. Of course the very idea of his climbing the stairs to her little flat to look at the cat was ridiculous. As though he had the slightest interest…

She buried her hot face in the filing cabinet. Never, *never*, she vowed, would she make that mistake again.

Dr Fforde, watching her, wondered how best to explain to her that visiting her at the flat would cause gossip—friendly, no doubt, but to be avoided. He decided to say nothing, but asked her in his usual grave way to telephone the hospital and say that he might be half an hour late.

'Mrs Seward has an appointment after the last patient. She is not a patient, so please show her in at once.'

The last patient had barely been shown out when Mrs Seward arrived. She was tall, slender, with a lovely face, skilfully made up, and wearing the kind of clothes Loveday dreamed of. She had a lovely smile, too.

'Hello—you're new, aren't you? What's happened to Miss Priss? Has Andrew finished? I'm a bit early.'

'Mrs Seward? Dr Fforde's expecting you.'

Loveday opened his door and stood aside for Mrs Seward to go in. Before she closed it she heard him say, 'Margaret—this is delightful.'

'Andrew, it's been so long...' was Mrs Seward's happy reply.

Loveday went back to her desk and got out the afternoon patients' notes. That done, she entered their names and phone numbers into the daily diary. It was time for her to go to her lunch, but she supposed that she should stay; they would go presently and she could lock up. He would be at the hospital during the afternoon, and there were no more patients until almost four o'clock.

She didn't have long to wait. They came out together presently, and the doctor stopped at the desk and asked her to lock up. 'And since the first patient is at four o'clock there's no need for you to come back until three.'

His voice was as kind as his smile. Mrs Seward smiled too. On their way down to the car she said, 'I like your receptionist. A mouse with green eyes.'

The extra hour or so for lunch wasn't to be ignored. Loveday gobbled a sandwich, fed Sam, and went shopping, returning with her own simple needs and weighed down by tins of cat food and more books. She had seen that the funny little shop squeezed in between the grocer and the butcher sold just about everything and had noticed some small, cheap radios. On pay day, she promised herself, she would buy one. And the greengrocer had had a bucketful of chrysanthemums outside his shop; they perhaps weren't quite as fresh as they might have been, but they would add a cheerful splash of colour in the flat.

The doctor arrived back five minutes before his patient, accepted the cup of tea she offered him and, when the last patient of the afternoon had gone, bade her goodnight without loss of time.

'They'll go out this evening,' said Loveday aloud. 'To one of those restaurants with little lamps on the tables. And then they'll go dancing. She's quite beautiful. They make a handsome pair.'

She locked up with her usual care and went upstairs to give Sam his supper and herself a pot of tea. She would have a pleasant evening, she told herself: an omelette for her supper and then a peaceful hour with one of the second-hand books.

'I'm becoming an old maid,' said Loveday.

There was news of Miss Priss in the morning; her mother was recovering from her stroke but must stay in hospital for another ten days. After that she would return home and be nursed by Miss Priss and a helper. There was every chance that she would recover, and then Miss Priss would be able to return to work once arrangements for her mother's comfort could be made.

The doctor told Loveday this without going into details, and although she was sorry for Miss Priss and her mother, she couldn't help feeling relief. She had known that sooner or later Miss Priss would be back, but the longer she could stay the more money she could save, and with some experience and a reference from the doctor she would have a better chance of finding work. She must remember, she told herself, to curb her tongue and not talk about herself or Sam.

As a result of this resolution the doctor was at first faintly amused and then puzzled at her wooden politeness towards him. She had become in the short time she had been working for him almost as efficient as Miss Priss; she was discreet, pleasantly attentive to his patients, willing to come early and work late if need be, and disappeared to her little flat so quietly that he barely noticed her going. And always there when he arrived in the mornings. It was what he expected and what he paid her for, but all the same he now had a vague sense of disquiet, so that he found himself thinking about her very frequently.

A few days later she went down rather earlier; there were more patients than usual today. The doctor would expect everything to be ready for them.

There was a man on the landing outside the consulting rooms, standing easily, hands in pockets, looking out of the landing window. He turned round to look at her as she reached the door.

He smiled at her and said good morning. 'I hoped someone would come soon. I'd love a cup of coffee.' At her surprised look, he added, 'Oh, it's quite all right, Andrew won't mind.'

When she still stood there, looking at him, he added impatiently, 'Open up, dear girl.'

'Certainly not,' said Loveday. 'I don't know who you

are, and even if you told me I'm not to know whether it's the truth. I'm so sorry, but if you want to see the doctor then you should come back at nine o'clock.'

She put the key in the lock. 'I have no intention of letting you in.'

She whisked herself inside, locked the door again and left him there. He had been sure of himself, demanding coffee, behaving as if he knew the doctor, but he could so easily be intent on skulduggery...

She set about her morning chores and had everything just as the doctor liked and the coffee ready when he came in.

The young man was with him and they were both laughing.

The doctor's good morning was said in his usual quiet manner, but his companion told Loveday, 'You see, I am a bona fide caller. Are you not remorseful at your treatment of me? And I only asked to be let in and given coffee.'

'You could have been a thief,' said Loveday.

'Quite right, Loveday,' interposed the doctor. 'You did the right thing and, since my cousin hasn't the good grace to introduce himself, I must do it for him. Charles Fforde, this is Miss Loveday West, who is my most efficient receptionist.'

Charles offered a hand, and after a tiny pause she shook it.

'What happened to Miss Prissy?'

'I'll tell you about her. Come into my room. There is time for coffee, but you must go away before my patients arrive.' The doctor opened his door. 'I should be free about one o'clock; we'll have lunch together.'

Loveday fetched the coffee. Charles was much

younger than the doctor—more her own age, she supposed. He was good-looking too, and well dressed. She thought uneasily that he was very like Miss Cattell's men-friends, only younger. On the other hand he was the doctor's cousin, and he, in her view, was beyond reproach.

Charles didn't stay long, and on his way out he paused by her desk.

'Did anyone ever tell you that you have very beautiful eyes? The rest of you is probably charming, though hardly breathtaking, but the eyes…!'

He bent down and kissed the end of her nose.

'Till we meet again,' he told her, and reached the door in time to hold it open for the first patient.

No one had ever told Loveday that her eyes were beautiful. She savoured that for the rest of the day and tried to forget his remark about not being breathtaking. It had been so long since anyone had passed a remark about her appearance that she found it hard to ignore.

That evening, getting ready for bed, she examined her face carefully. 'Hardly breathtaking' was a kind way of saying plain…

All the same she took extra pains with her face and hair in the morning, and made plans to buy a new dress on Saturday afternoon.

If she had hoped to see Charles the next day she was disappointed. There was no sign of him, and Dr Fforde, beyond his usual pleasant greeting, had nothing to say. All the same, she spent Saturday afternoon searching for a dress. It had to be something that would last. She found it after much searching: a navy blue wool crêpe, well cut and elegant, with the kind of neckline which could be dressed up by a pretty scarf. She bore it back and tried it on with Sam for a rather bored audience.

And on Monday morning she wore it to work.

Dr Fforde, wishing her his usual pleasant good morning noticed it immediately. It was undoubtedly suitable for her job, but it hardly enhanced her appearance. Her pretty mousy hair and those green eyes should be complemented by rich greens and russet, not buried in navy blue. He thought it unlikely that she had many friends, and perhaps none close enough to point this out to her. A pity. He sat down at his desk and started to go through his post.

It was Charles who voiced this same opinion when he came again during the week. He sauntered in after the last of the morning patients had gone and stopped at her desk.

'A new dress', he said as he eyed her up and down in a friendly fashion. 'In excellent taste too, dear girl, but why hide your charms behind such a middle-aged colour? You should be wearing pink and blue and emerald-green, and all the colours of the rainbow…'

'Not if she is to remain my receptionist,' said the doctor from his door, so that Loveday's wide smile at the sight of Charles was quenched. She contrived to look faintly amused, although her eyes sparkled green fire. The phone rang then and she turned to answer it, and the two men went into the consulting room together.

She had been delighted to see Charles, and although he didn't like the new dress he had said it was hiding her charms—which sounded old-fashioned but pleasant. And then Dr Fforde had to spoil it all. Who knew what Charles would have said if they had been left alone?

Loveday, a level-headed girl, realised that she was behaving in a way quite unlike her usual self-contained self. 'Which won't do,' she muttered as the phone rang again. And no one could have looked more efficient and at the same time inconspicuous than she did as Dr Fforde and Charles came into the room again.

'I shall be at the hospital until five o'clock,' the doctor told her. 'Have the afternoon off, but please be here by half past four.'

So Loveday had a leisurely lunch and decided to do some more shopping. She didn't need much, but she seldom had the chance to go out during the day and it was a bright day even if chilly. She got into her jacket—navy blue again, and bought to last—and with her shopping basket over one arm went out.

She had only gone a few yards down the street when she met Charles.

He took her arm. 'How about a walk in the park and tea? It's a splendid afternoon for exercise.'

She didn't try to conceal her pleasure at seeing him again. 'It sounds lovely, but I'm going shopping.'

'You can shop any day of the week.' He had tucked one arm into hers. 'Half an hour's brisk walk, then tea, and then if you must shop...'

'I have to be back by half past four.'

'Yes, yes. That's almost three hours away.'

He was laughing at her and, despite her good resolutions, she smiled back. 'A walk would be nice...'

He was an amusing companion and, bored with having nothing much to do for the moment, he found it intriguing to attract this rather sedate girl who had no idea how to make the most of herself. He had charm and a light-hearted way of talking, uncaring that he rarely meant a word of what he uttered. Those who knew him well joined in his cheerful banter and didn't take it seriously, but Loveday wasn't to know that...

He took her to a small café near the park, plied her with cream cakes and called her dear girl, and when they parted outside the consulting rooms he begged her to see him again. He touched the tip of her nose very gently as he spoke and his smile was such that she agreed at once.

'But I'm only free on Saturday afternoons and Sundays.'

'Sunday it shall be. We will drive into the country and walk and talk and eat at some village pub.' He turned away. 'Ten o'clock?'

'He didn't wait for her reply, which just for a moment she found disturbing, but she brushed that aside. A day out in his company would be lovely.

Dr Fforde, coming back just before five o'clock, wondered what had given Loveday a kind of inner glow; she was no longer insignificant, and her ordinary face was alight with happiness.

He asked, 'You enjoyed your afternoon?'

'Yes, thank you, Doctor.' Her beaming smile included him in her happiness, and for some reason that made him uneasy.

At breakfast on Sunday morning, Loveday explained to Sam that she would be away for the day. 'Well, most of it, I hope.' She added, 'But I won't be late home.' She kissed his elderly head. 'Be a good boy.'

Charles had said a drive into the country and a village pub. Her jacket and a skirt would be quite suitable; she would wear her good shoes and the pale blue sweater...

She was ready and waiting when she heard the silence of the quiet street disturbed by the prolonged blowing of his car's horn. She reached his car just as he was about to blow it again. 'Oh, hush,' she begged him. 'It's Sunday morning.'

He had looked faintly impatient, but now he laughed. 'So it is and we have the whole day before us.' He leaned across and opened the car door. 'Jump in.'

His car was a sports model, scarlet and flashy. She suppressed the instant thought that Dr Fforde's car was more to her liking and settled down beside Charles.

'It's a lovely morning,' she began.

'Marvellous, darling, but don't chatter until we are out of London.'

So she sat quietly, happy just to be there, sitting beside him, leaving the streets and rows of houses behind for a few hours.

He drove south, through Sevenoaks, and she wondered where they were going. They were well clear of London by now, but he had nothing much to say until he asked suddenly, 'Have you any idea where we're going?'

'No, except that it's south—towards the coast.'

'Brighton, darling. Plenty to do and see there.'

She had expected a day in the country—he had mentioned a country pub. Surely Brighton wasn't much different from London? But what did it matter where they went? She was happy in his company and he made her laugh...

He parked at the seafront and they had coffee and then walked, first by the sea and then through the town, stopping to look at the shop windows in the Lanes. Charles promised her that the next time they came he would take her to the Pavilion. They had lunch in a fashionable pub and then walked again, and if it wasn't quite what she had expected it didn't really matter. She was having a lovely day out and Charles was a delightful companion, teasing her a little, letting her see that he liked her, and telling her that he had never met a girl quite like her before. Loveday, hopelessly ignorant of the fashionable world, believed every word of it.

They drove back to London after a splendid tea in one of the seafront hotels.

'Do you come here often?' Loveday wanted to know.

Charles gave her his charming smile. 'Never with such a delightful companion.' He might have added, And only because here I'm most unlikely to meet anyone I know. He wasn't doing any harm, he told himself. Loveday led a dull life; what could be kinder than to give her a taste of romance? And it would keep him amused for the next few weeks…

She was a dear little thing, he reflected as they drove back, but too quiet and dull for him. It amused him to see how she blossomed under his attention.

'We must do this again,' he told her. 'I'll be away next weekend, but there's a good film we might go to see one evening. Wednesday. I'll come for you about half past seven.'

'I'd like that, thank you,' she said. And, Loveday being Loveday, she added, 'I won't need to dress up? I haven't anything smart to wear.'

'No, no. You look very nice.'

He turned his head to smile at her. She was wearing something dull and unflattering, but the cinema he had in mind was well away from his usual haunts and he wasn't likely to see anyone who knew him.

He didn't get out of the car when they got back, but kissed her cheek and told her what a marvellous day it had been and then drove away before she had the key in the door. He had cut things rather fine; he had barely an hour in which to change for the evening.

Loveday climbed the stairs to the flat, to be met by an impatient Sam. She fed him and made a pot of tea before sitting down to drink it while she told him about her day. 'He's so nice,' she told Sam. 'He makes me laugh, and he makes me feel pretty and amusing although I know I'm not. We're going out again on Wednesday evening and I wish I had some pretty clothes to wear. He said it doesn't matter but I'd like to look my best for him. He notices what I'm wearing.' She sighed. 'Dr Fforde doesn't even see me—not as a girl, that is, only as his receptionist. And why I should think of him, I don't know.'

She was wrong, of course. Dr Fforde, coming to his rooms on Monday morning, at once saw the inner glow in Loveday's face and the sparkle in her eyes.

CHAPTER THREE

THE doctor bade her good morning and paused long enough to ask her if she had had a good weekend. 'You have friends to visit?' he wanted to know.

'Me? No. I hadn't time to make friends when I was with Miss Cattell,' she told him cheerfully.

So who or what had given her ordinary face that happy look? He went into his consulting room, thinking about it. It would hardly do for him to ask her how she spent her spare time, although he had a strong inclination to know that. Besides, it would be difficult to ask because her manner towards him had a distinct tinge of reserve. Probably she thought him too elderly to have an interest in her private life. A man approaching forty must seem middle-aged to a girl in her twenties.

He sat down to open his post and glanced up briefly when she came in with his coffee. The happy look was still there…

It seemed to Loveday that Wednesday took a long time in coming, and when it did she was in a fever of impatience; the last patient of the afternoon was elderly, nervous and inclined to want her own way, demanding a good deal of attention from the nurse and then sitting down again to repeat her symptoms once again to a patient Dr Fforde.

It was long after five when Loveday ushered her out, and it was almost an hour later when the nurse and Dr Fforde had gone too and she was at last ready to leave herself.

She sped up to the flat, fed an impatient Sam, made tea for herself and gobbled a sandwich left over from her lunch. She was hungry, but that was a small price to pay for an evening with Charles. She showered, changed into the jacket, skirt and a cream silk blouse, did her face with unusual care, brushed her mousy hair smooth and decided against her only hat. At least her shoes and handbag were good, even if they were no longer new.

She glanced out of the window; he would be here at any moment and he had been impatient on Sunday. She gave Sam a hug, locked up and hurried down to the street. She was just in time as Charles drew up.

He leaned over and opened the car door. 'There you are, darling. How clever of you to know that I hate being kept waiting.' When she had settled into the seat beside him he dropped a careless kiss on her cheek. She really was quite a taking little thing; it was a pity she dressed in such a dull fashion.

The film was just released, a triumph of modern cinema and Loveday, who hadn't been to the cinema for a long time, enjoyed it. When it ended and they had reached his car her heart lifted when he said, 'A drink and something to eat? It's still early.'

Eleven o'clock at night was late for her, now that she no longer had to keep the erratic hours Miss Cattell's

household were obliged to put up with, and she had
been going to her bed well before eleven. But she cast
good sense to the winds and agreed.

To be disappointed. She was hungry, but Charles, it
seemed, had dined earlier that evening, so 'drinks' were
indifferent coffee and a bowl of nuts and tiny cheese
biscuits in the bar of a nearby hotel. Not the usual hotel
Charles frequented, and he made no attempt to dally
over them. Loveday could see that he was anxious to
be gone, and since she was by now as attracted to him
as he had intended, she declared that she should go
back to the flat.

'It's been a lovely evening,' she told him, 'and thank
you for taking me.'

'My dearest girl, the pleasure was all mine.' He
stopped before the consulting rooms, leaned across to
open her door and then put an arm around her to kiss
her. A sweet little thing, he reflected, but he was
becoming the littlest bit bored with her. All the same
he said, 'We must have another day out soon.'

He drove off, leaving her on the pavement. Loveday,
unlocking the door, told herself that he must have had
an urgent reason to rush away like that, and drowned
the thought in the prospect of another day out with
him.

'I have never been so happy,' she told Sam, eating
her late supper of scrambled eggs on toast. And she was
sure that she was. A nameless, niggling doubt at the
back of her mind was easily lost in the remembrance
of his kiss.

She made a mistake in the case notes in the morning,
and forgot to give Dr Fforde a message from the
hospital. Not an urgent one, but all the same there had

been no excuse for forgetting it—except that she had been thinking of Charles.

The doctor accepted her apology with a nod and said nothing, but back in his home that evening he sat for a long time thinking about it.

Loveday was very careful during the next few days not to make any more mistakes. Never mind her vague dreams of a blissful future; the present was reality—security, a roof over her head, money in her pocket. Her scrupulous attention to her duties and her anxiety to please the doctor he found at first amusing, then puzzling. He didn't pretend to himself that he wasn't interested in her, but he was a man of no conceit and found it unlikley that a girl of her age, even if she was as level-headed as Loveday was, would wish to make a friend of a man so much older than she. He could only hope that whoever it was who had brought that look into her face would make her happy.

Charles phoned one morning during the week. Loveday had the place ready, the coffee set for the doctor and everything prepared for the day's work.

'Darling,' said Charles over the phone, 'I thought we might have a lovely evening on Saturday. Wear a pretty dress; we'll dine and dance.'

He hung up before she could reply.

It seemed that Saturday would never come. When it did she got up early and went down to the consulting rooms; she set everything to rights ready for Monday before hurrying to get a bus which would take her to Oxford Street.

She had raided her nest egg, shutting her eyes to the fact that she was making a great hole in her secure future, but no one—no man—had ever asked her out to dine and dance before, and certainly not a man such as Charles, so full of fun and so obviously liking her a lot, perhaps even loving her...

It took her an hour or two to find what she wanted; a plain sheath of a dress, and well cut, although the material from which it was made was cheap—but the colour was right: a pale bronze which gave her hair colour and flattered her eyes. There was also money enough for shoes, found after much searching on a bargain rail in a cheap shoe shop. They weren't leather, though they looked as though they were, and they went well with the dress.

She hurried back home with her purchases to give Sam his tea before she boiled an egg and made a pot of tea for herself. Then she began to get ready for the evening. It was a pity that Charles hadn't said at what time he would call for her...

She was ready far too soon, and sat peering out of the window into the street below. Perhaps he had forgotten...

It was almost eight o'clock when she saw his car stop before the house, and Loveday, being Loveday, with no thought of keeping him waiting or playing hard to get, flew down to the door.

He was sitting in the car, waiting for her, and because she was living for the moment in a delightful dream world of her own his casual manners were unnoticed. She got into the car beside him and he put an arm round her and kissed her lightly.

'Got that pretty dress?' he wanted to know, and looked doubtfully at her coat; it was plain and serviceable and obviously not in the height of fashion.

'Yes.' She smiled at him. 'I bought it this morning.'

He had planned the evening carefully: dinner at a small restaurant in Chelsea—smart enough to impress her but hardly likely to entertain anyone he might know—and afterwards there was a dance hall not too far away. It was hardly a place he would consider taking any of his acquaintances, but he suspected that to Loveday it would be the highlight of their evening.

Their table was in the corner of the restaurant, a pleasant enough place, with shaded lights and its dozen or so tables already filled. The food was good too, and he ordered champagne. She could have sat there for ever opposite him, listening to his amusing talk, smiling happily at his admiring glances, but they didn't linger over dinner.

'I'm longing to dance with you,' Charles told her.

The dance floor was crowded and very noisy, and hemmed in by other dancers, they scarcely moved. For that Loveday was secretly thankful, as her opportunities to go dancing had been non-existent at Miss Cattell's home. She was disappointed but not surprised when he declared impatiently that dancing was quite out of the question.

'A pity,' he told her as they left the place. 'Having to cut short a delightful evening.'

There would be other evenings, thought Loveday, and waited for him to say so, only he didn't. Indeed, he didn't mention seeing her again as he drove her back. He was unusually silent, and once or twice she thought that he was on the point of telling her something.

'Is there anything the matter?' she asked.

'Matter? What on earth put that idea into your head?' He sounded angry, but then a moment later said,

'Sorry, darling, I didn't mean to snap. I wanted this evening to be something special.'

He stopped outside the consulting rooms and turned to look at her. 'You wouldn't like to ask me up?'

'No, I wouldn't.' She smiled at him, and he put an arm round her shoulders and kissed her, then leaned forward to open her door.

She got out and turned to look at him. 'It was a lovely evening, Charles, thank you.' She waited for him to say something as she closed the door. But all he did was lift a hand in farewell and drive off. She stood on the pavement for a moment, disappointed that he hadn't said when they would meet again, and vaguely disturbed about it, but the memory of his kiss blotted uneasiness away. She unlocked the door and let herself into the house.

Dr Fforde, wanting some notes he had left in his consulting room, had walked round from his house, found them, put out his desk light, and was on his way through the waiting room when the sound of a car outside sent him to the window. He stood there, watching Loveday get out of the car, Charles drive away and her stillness before she turned to go into the house. He went then to open the door and switch on the landing light.

'Loveday.' His voice was reassuringly normal. 'I came to collect some notes I needed. 'I'm on my way out.'

He came down the stairs, switching on lights as he came, and found her standing in the hall.

'I've been out,' said Loveday unnecessarily, and added for good measure, 'With Charles.'

'Yes, I saw you and the car from the window. You've had a pleasant evening?'

She smiled at him. She would have liked to have told him all about her and Charles. He was, she reflected, the kind of person you wanted to tell things to. Instead she said happily, 'Oh, I had a lovely time,' and then, because she wanted to make it all quite clear, 'Charles has taken me out several times—we—seem to get on well together.'

Dr Fforde put his hand on the door. He smiled, but all he said was, 'Sleep well!'

In the flat, she told Sam all about it. 'I'm not sure if Dr Fforde likes me going out with Charles. He's too nice to say so…'

She hung the pretty dress away and wondered when she would wear it again. Soon, she hoped.

She was used to being lonely. Sunday passed happily enough, with attending church and a walk, then back to Sam's company and the Sunday papers. Monday couldn't come quickly enough—there was sure to be a phone call from Charles. She counted her money once again. Perhaps a long skirt and a pretty top would be an asset? Something she could wear which wasn't too noticeable? They would probably go dancing again, somewhere quieter—the dance hall hadn't been the kind of place Charles would normally visit, she thought, but of course it had been near the restaurant.

Her spirits dwindled with the passing days. She went about her work quietly, careful not to make mistakes, passed the time of day with Nurse, answered the doctor when he spoke to her in her usual quiet way, but by the end of the week the happiness he had seen in her face was subdued.

It was on Thursday evening after the last patient had gone that he called her into his consulting rooms.

He was standing by the window looking down into the street below. He said over his shoulder. 'Loveday, there is something you should know…'

Miss Priss was coming back! She swallowed a sudden rush of feelings and said politely, 'Yes, Doctor?'

He turned to look at her. He said in a harsh voice, 'Charles is to be married in two weeks…his fiancée has been in America. You are unaware of this?'

She nodded, and then said, 'If you don't mind, I'd like to go to the flat. I'll clear up later.' Her voice didn't sound quite like hers, but it was almost steady. On no account must she burst into tears or scream that she didn't believe him. Dr Fforde wasn't a man to tell lies— lies to turn her world upside down.

He didn't speak, but opened the door for her. And when she looked up at him and whispered, 'Thank you,' from a pale face, the kindness of his smile almost overset her.

She let herself into the flat and, almost unaware of what she was doing, fed Sam, made tea and sat down to drink it. This was a nightmare from which she would presently wake, she told herself. She was still sitting there, the tea cold in front of her, Sam looking anxious on her lap, when the flat door opened and Dr Fforde came in.

'I have a key,' he observed. 'I think you will feel better if you talk about it.' He glanced at the tea. 'We will have tea together and while we drink it we can discuss the matter.'

He put the kettle on and made fresh tea, found clean cups and saucers and put a nicely laid tray on the table between them. Loveday, watching him wordlessly, felt surprise at the ease with which he performed the small household duty.

He poured the tea and put a cup in front of her. 'Tell me about it—Charles has been taking you out? You began to feel that he was falling in love with you?' He added, 'Drink your tea.'

She sipped obediently. There was no reason why she should answer him, for this was her own business, none of his, and yet she heard herself say meekly, 'Not very often. Once or twice to the cinema and a day in the country and last Saturday evening.' She said in a voice thick with tears, 'I've been a silly fool, haven't I?'

'No,' he said gently. 'How were you to know if Charles didn't tell you? I don't suppose he deliberately set out to hurt you. He has fallen in and out of love many times, but he is to marry a strong-minded American girl who will make sure that he loves only her. He was having a last fling. He has been selfish and uncaring and has probably already forgotten you. That sounds harsh, but the obvious thing is to forget him, too. Believe me, you will, even though at the moment you don't believe me.'

Loveday wiped her hands across her wet eyes like a child. 'How could I have been so stupid? You have only to look at me. I'm not even a little bit pretty and I wear all the wrong clothes.' She suddenly began to cry again. 'I bought that dress just for the evening because he said I ought to wear pretty colours!' She gulped and sniffed. 'Please will you go away now?'

'No. Go and wash your face and do your hair and get a coat. We will have our supper together.' He glanced at his watch. 'Mrs Duckett, my housekeeper, will have it ready in half an hour or so. You will eat everything put before you and then I shall bring you back here and you will go straight to bed and sleep. In the morning your heart will be sore, and perhaps a little cracked, but not broken.'

He sounded so kind that she wanted to weep again. 'I'm not hungry…' But all the same she went to the bedroom and did her hair, and the best she could with her poor pink-nosed face and puffy eyelids. Presently she went back to where he was waiting, the tea things tidied away and Sam on his knee.

She hadn't expected the house in the mews, a rather larger one than its neighbours, with windows on either side of its front door flanked by little bay trees. He ushered her into the narrow hall and Mrs Duckett came to meet them.

'This is my receptionist, Miss Loveday West,' said the doctor. 'She has had an upsetting experience and it seemed to me that one of your splendid suppers would make her feel better, Mrs Duckett. Loveday, this is my housekeeper, Mrs Duckett.'

Loveday shook hands and the housekeeper gave her a motherly look. Been crying her eyes out, by the look of it, she reflected, and took the coat the doctor had taken from Loveday.

'Ten minutes or so.' She beamed at them both. 'Just nice time for a drop of sherry.'

The doctor opened the door and pushed Loveday gently ahead of him. The room had a window at each end and there was a cheerful fire burning in the elegant fireplace between them. It was a charming room, with sofas on each side of the hearth, a Pembroke table between them and several bookshelves crowded with books. There was a long-case clock in one corner, and the whole room was lighted by shaded lamps on the various small tables.

'Come by the fire,' said the doctor. 'Do you like dogs?'

When she nodded she saw two beady eyes peering from a shock of hair, watching her from a basket by a winged armchair by the window.

'A dog—he's yours?'

'Yes. He stays in his basket because he's been hurt.' Dr Fforde bent to stroke the tousled head. 'He got knocked down in the street and no one owns him.'

'You'll keep him?'

'Why not? He's a splendid fellow and will be perfectly fit in a week or so.' He had poured sherry and offered her a glass. 'He has two broken legs. They're in plaster.'

'May I stroke him?'

'Of course. I don't think he's had much kindness in his life so far.'

Loveday knelt by the basket and offered a hand, and then gently ran it over the dog's rough coat. 'He's lovely. What do you call him?'

'Can you think of a suitable name? I have had him only a couple of days.'

She thought about it, aware that beneath this fragile conversation about the dog there was hidden a great well of unhappiness which at any minute threatened to overflow.

'Something that sounds friendly—you know, like a family dog with a lot of children.' She paused, thinking that sounded like nonsense. 'Bob or Bertie or Rob.'

'We will call him Bob. Come and finish your sherry and we'll have our supper.'

She wished Bob goodbye, and he stuck out a pink tongue and licked the back of her hand. 'Oh, I do hope he'll get well quickly,' said Loveday.

She had expected supper to be a light evening meal, but it wasn't supper at all. It was dinner at its best, eaten in a small dining room, sitting on Hepplewhite chairs at a table covered with a damask cloth and set with silver and glass. There was soup from a Coalport soup plate, chicken, cooked deliciously in a wine sauce, potato purée and tiny sprouts, and one of Mrs Duckett's sherry trifles to follow.

The doctor poured a crisp white wine and maintained a steady flow of undemanding talk, giving her no chance to think about anything other than polite answers. They had coffee at the table before he drove her back to the consulting rooms, went up to the flat with her, switched on the lights, wished Sam an affable goodnight and went back down the stairs after bidding her a quiet goodnight. She tried to stammer out her thanks but he waved them aside.

'I'll see you in the morning, Loveday,' he told her. 'Go to bed and go to sleep.'

And, strangely enough, that was what she did. She woke early, though, and her unhappiness, held at bay the evening before, took over. But now, in the light of the morning, she was able to think about it with a degree of good sense. She saw now that she had behaved like a lovesick teenager—just the kind of silly girl Charles had needed to keep him amused while his future wife was away.

That didn't make her unhappiness any the less. She had her dreams and she had been carried away by what she had supposed was Charles's delight in her

company. She told herself that it was because she had
been so little in a man's company that she had mistaken
his attentions for real feeling. This was a sensible con-
clusion, which none the less didn't stop her crying her
eyes out, so that she had to spend a long time doing
things to her face before she went down to the consulting rooms.

She thought she had made rather a good job of it as
she studied her face in the large mirror between the
windows in the waiting room, but it was a good thing
that she couldn't read the doctor's thoughts as he came
in.

He noted the puffed eyelids and the still pink nose
and the resolutely smiling mouth and reflected that she
had one of the most unassuming faces he had ever seen.
Except for those glorious eyes, of course. So what was
it about her that took so much of his interest? An
interest which he had felt the first time he had met
her…

He went to his consulting room, accepted the coffee
she brought him, and considered the matter. He was in
love with her, of course; it was not a passing fancy. He
had over the years considered marrying, and had, like
any other man, fancied himself in love from time to
time. But he had always known that the girl in question
hadn't been the right one, that sooner or later he would
meet a woman whom he would love and want to have
for his wife. But now was hardly the time to tell
Loveday that. Patience was called for, and he had plenty
of that.

He had a busy day ahead of him, and would be
spending the greater part of it at the hospital, so beyond
giving Loveday instructions about patients and the time

of his return, he had nothing to say. He could see that she was determined to keep her feelings concealed.

Only that evening, as he left to go home, he paused at her desk, where she was still busy.

'Bob spent half an hour in the garden this morning. You would be surprised at what he can manage to do on two legs and with a lot of help.'

She said gravely, 'He is a darling dog. I think he will be devoted to you; you saved his life.'

He smiled down at her. 'I think he will be a fine fellow once he is well again. Goodnight, Loveday.'

It was quiet after he had gone. It would be absurd, she told herself, to say that she missed him. She finished the tidying up and went upstairs to Sam's welcoming voice. She had got through the day, hadn't she? she reflected, and if she could get through one day she could get through as many more as she must before she could finally forget Charles.

The following week seemed endless; she listened to Nurse's confidences concerning her boyfriend with sympathy, presented a welcoming face to the doctor's patients, and carried on long one-sided conversations with Sam.

She planned her weekend with him. 'I shall go shopping on Saturday afternoon,' she told him, 'and on Sunday I'll go to church in the morning and then to Hyde Park in the afternoon, and we'll have a cosy evening together.'

And Sam, grown comfortably stout and placid, got onto her lap and went to sleep. Life for him, at any rate, was quite perfect.

The last of Friday afternoon's patients came late. Nurse was annoyed because that meant she couldn't leave punctually, and just before the patient was ushered out the phone rang. Five minutes later Dr Fforde left too.

He bade the nurse goodnight, told Loveday to lock up and that he would be at the hospital, and went away.

Nurse followed him almost at once, grumbling because she would have to rush home and change before going out for the evening. 'And I wanted to get my hair done,' she complained, slamming the door behind her.

Which left Loveday alone, putting things to rights. She would be down in the morning to make sure that everything was ready for Monday, but all the same she liked to leave the place just so. She didn't hurry for she had no reason to do so, and even though after a week her unhappiness was dulled, her solitary evenings were the most difficult part of the day.

She spent longer than she needed in the consulting rooms the next morning, keeping her mind resolutely on prosaic things such as her shopping list and Monday's patients. The phone rang several times too— patients wanting to make appointments—and just as she was about to lock up, Mrs Seward rang.

'I know Fforde isn't there,' she told Loveday, 'but would you leave a message for him? Ask him to come and see me on Monday if he can manage it? If he knows before his morning patients he may be able to arrange something. Thank you. Am I talking to the girl with the green eyes?'

'Yes.'

'Miss Priss not back yet? I'm sure you're filling her shoes very competently. You won't forget the message?'

She rang off and Loveday thought what a pleasant, friendly voice she had. Perhaps the doctor was going to marry her...

She was on the way upstairs to her flat when she heard the front door bang shut. It wouldn't be Todd, he used the entrance at the back of the house, and the three other medical men who had rooms there were all out of London for the weekend, Todd had told her that before he had gone home the previous evening.

Not quite frightened, but cautious, Loveday started down the stairs.

Dr Fforde was coming up them, two at a time. He stood on the landing, looking up at her.

'I'm glad I find you in,' he observed. 'Can you spare an hour later on today? Late afternoon, perhaps? I'll call for you around four o'clock. Bob is doing splendidly, but I fancy he needs some distraction—a new face. Will you come?'

'Well, if you think it might help him to get better quickly... He can't go out?'

'Into the garden. With two of us he might feel encouraged to hobble around in his plasters. He has forgotten how to enjoy life. Indeed, I think that he never had that opportunity.'

'Oh, the poor dog. Of course I'll come.'

'Good!' He was already going back downstairs. 'I'll see you later.'

'Oh, wait!' cried Loveday. 'I almost forgot. Mrs Seward phoned. She asked if you would arrange to see her on Monday; she wanted you to know as soon as possible when you got here on Monday morning.'

He nodded, said, 'Thanks,' and went on his way out of the house.

There would be no time to sit and brood; Loveday fed Sam, had a quick lunch, and hurried to the shops. They knew her there by now, with her modest purchases of lamb chops and sausages, tins of cat food, butter, tea and coffee, some greengrocery and a loaf and, last of all, another book or two. A nice, quiet little lady they told each other, and occasionally they popped something extra into her basket.

She went back in good time to do her hair and her face, and leave the ever-hungry Sam something to eat on his saucer, before going to the window to watch for the doctor's car. When it came, instead of waiting there for her to go down, he got out and came into the house and all the way to her flat to knock on her door.

She couldn't help but compare his easy good manners with Charles's careless ones, and a small shaft of pleasure shot through her as he ushered her into the car and closed the door.

Bob was pleased to see her, and instead of lying rather listlessly in his basket he made valiant efforts to sit up.

'Oh, you clever boy,' said Loveday. 'You're better! He is better?' she asked anxiously.

'Yes. The vet's pleased with him. It wasn't only the legs, he was in poor shape, but now he's getting his strength back. We'll go into the garden for a few minutes and you can see what he can do.'

The doctor carried the little dog outside and set him down gently, and after a few moments Bob dragged himself onto his two front legs. He wasn't sure what to do with the ungainly plastered back legs, but presently he stood, a bit wobbly, looking pleased with himself.

'Once he's discovered that he can use his legs

without pain, even if they're clumsy, there'll be no holding him.' The doctor picked him up and carried him back indoors and settled Loveday in a chair by the fire.

'Shall we have tea? Bob loves company.'

Mrs Duckett's teas were like no other: there were muffins in a silver dish, tiny sandwiches, fairy cakes, and a cake thick with fruit and nuts. It was just the right meal for a chilly autumn day, sitting round the fire, talking of this and that, both of them perfectly at ease.

Dr Fforde, who was skilled in the art of extracting information from patients who were reluctant to give it, went to work on Loveday.

'No family?' he enquired casually. 'Surely someone—an aunt or uncle or cousin—even if you have little to do with them?'

He was an easy man to talk to. 'I was brought up by an aunt; she died some years ago. There's another aunt—my father's much older sister. She lives in a village on the edge of Dartmoor. We send each other cards at Christmas but I've never met her. I—I haven't liked to ask her if I might go and see her. I expect she thinks I have a satisfactory life here, and it's a long way. In any case, Miss Cattell didn't like me having a holiday. I hated being there, but it was a job, and I'm not trained for anything, am I?'

He agreed in a non-committal way. 'I have no doubt that you would have no difficulty in getting work. There is always a shortage of good receptionists. But you would like to visit your aunt?'

'Yes. Well, I mean, she is family, isn't she? If you see what I mean? But I expect she's happy living in Devon and would hate to have her life disrupted, even for a brief visit.' She added, 'And I'm very happy here.'

He was looking at her so thoughtfully that she hurried to change the subject. 'This is a charming house. You must like coming home each day.'

'Indeed I do, but I'm fond of the country too. I don't know Dartmoor at all; it must be very different…'

The casualness of his remark encouraged her to say, 'Oh, I'm sure it is. My aunt lives in a small village, somewhere near Ashburton. Buckland-in-the-Moor. It sounds lovely, but I expect it's lonely. It's a long way away.'

The doctor, having obtained all the information he wanted, began to talk of Bob and his future, which led naturally enough to Sam, his intelligence, his appetite and his delightful company…

Loveday glanced at the clock. 'Heavens, it's almost six o'clock. If you don't mind, I'd like to go back to the flat. It's been lovely, but I've several things to do and the evenings go so quickly.'

Which wasn't true. They dragged from one hour to the next while she did her best to forget Charles's red car screaming to a halt below her window…

The doctor made no demur. She bade Bob goodbye, thanked the doctor for her tea and got back into the car. At the consulting rooms she began to say, 'You don't need to get out—'

She could have saved her breath; he went upstairs with her, opened the flat door and switched on the lights, and bade Sam a cheerful good evening before expressing, in the briefest manner, his thanks for her company.

'Bob was delighted to see you,' he assured her. He had been delighted too, but he wasn't going to say so.

Loveday, listening to his footsteps receding on the

stairs, was aware of a loneliness worse than usual. 'It's because he's such a large man that I notice when he's not here,' she told Sam.

CHAPTER FOUR

IT WAS on Monday morning that she saw the doctor had given himself a day off on Wednesday. She guessed why at once. It would be Charles's wedding day—a guess confirmed presently when Nurse came. She had a glossy magazine under one arm.

'Look at this.' She found the page and handed it to Loveday. 'Remember Dr Fforde's young cousin, who came here a few weeks ago? He's getting married—here's his picture and that's his fiancée. Pretty, isn't she? They are going to live in America, lucky them. The wedding is on Wednesday—a big one—you know, huge hats and white satin and bridesmaids. I must say they make a handsome pair.'

She took the magazine back again. 'Dr Fforde will go—he's bound to, isn't he? They're cousins, even if he is a lot older.'

'She's very pretty,' said Loveday, and wished that the phone would ring so that she had an excuse not to stand there gossiping. And the phone did ring, so that Nurse went away to the dressing room which was her workplace. Since there was a busy day ahead of them there would be little chance of more chatting. Loveday heaved a sigh of relief and turned a welcoming smile onto the first patient.

But, busy or not, it was hard not to keep thinking of Charles. She knew now that the whole thing had been nothing but an amusing interlude to him, and if she hadn't led such a narrow life she would have recognised that and treated the whole affair in the same light-hearted manner. But knowing that didn't make it any easier to forget...

On Tuesday the doctor was at the hospital all day, returning at five o'clock to see two patients in his consulting rooms. It had been very quiet all day, although Loveday had been kept busy enough making appointments. It had been a good opportunity to sort through the papers scattered on the doctor's desk, tidy them into heaps and write one or two reminder notes for him. Tomorrow he would be away all day, but since he had said nothing she supposed that she would be there as usual, taking calls and messages.

Neither patient stayed long, and it was barely six o'clock when she ushered the last one out and began to tidy up.

The doctor left soon after, but first he stopped to tell her that he had switched on the answering-machine. 'Anything urgent will be referred to Dr Gregg,' he told her, 'and you need only be here between ten o'clock and noon, then again between five o'clock and six. I'll be in as usual on Thursday.' He smiled suddenly. 'Would you do something for me? Would you go to my house in the early afternoon and give Bob half an hour in the garden? Mrs Duckett is nervous of hurting him. He's managing very well now, but he does need someone there.' He added, 'That is, unless you have planned something?'

'No, no. I haven't. Of course I'll go and keep Bob company for a little while. Mrs Duckett won't mind?'

'Mrs Duckett will be delighted. Goodnight, Loveday.'

She would do her weekly shopping in the morning, Loveday decided, and go to the doctor's house around two o'clock. She sat down to make out her small list of groceries. 'And a tin of sardines for you,' she promised Sam.

The doctor's house was a brisk ten minutes' walk away. Loveday knocked on its elegant front door just after two o'clock and was admitted by a smiling Mrs Duckett.

'Bob's waiting for you. I told him you'd be here soon. He misses the doctor when he's not home. I'm fond of him, but I'm a bit nervous on account of his legs. Keep your coat on, miss, it'll be chilly in the garden. Half an hour, the doctor said, and then you're to have a cup of tea before you go.'

She bustled Loveday into the sitting room. 'Look at that, then. He's trying to get onto his legs he's that happy to see you.'

She opened the doors onto the garden and trotted away with the reminder that tea would be brought at three o'clock.

Loveday knelt and put an arm round Bob's shoulders. Now that he was fed and rested and belonged to someone he was quite handsome, although his looks could be attributed to a variety of ancestors. Not that that mattered in the least, she assured him.

She picked him up and took him into the garden, and once there he took heart and struggled around, dragging his cumbersome plastered legs, obviously glad of her company. After a time they went back to the house and sat companionably side by side, he in his basket, Loveday on the floor beside him. He was a splendid companion too, listening with every sign of interest while she told him about Charles getting married and how lucky he was to have such a kind master, and presently Mrs Duckett came with the tea tray. There was dainty china and a little silver teapot, crumpets in a covered dish, little cakes and wafer-thin bread and butter, and, of course, a biscuit for Bob.

Loveday enjoyed every morsel and strangely enough she didn't think about the wedding, only that tea would have been even nicer if the doctor had been there with them.

She left soon after and hurried back to the consulting rooms, then sat at her desk from five o'clock until the clock struck six, answering a few calls on the phone and making sure that everything was ready for the morning.

The doctor arrived punctually the next morning, and paused on his way to thank her for visiting Bob, but if she had hoped for him to mention the wedding she was to be disappointed. With the remark that they had a busy morning before them, he went into his consulting room and closed the door.

Watching Sam scoff his supper that evening, she wondered aloud if she would be asked on Friday morning to visit Bob at the weekend, but here again she was to be disappointed; beyond reminding her that he would be at the hospital on Monday morning and wishing her a pleasant weekend he had nothing to say.

'And why I should have expected anything else I have no idea,' said Loveday, expressing her thoughts, as usual, to Sam.

The weather had changed, becoming dull and wet and windy. All the same, she wrapped up warmly and went walking. Not to the shops; she might spend too much money if she did that, and the nest egg in the Post Office was growing steadily. It would have been even larger if she hadn't bought that dress...

She was beginning to feel secure; there had been no news of Miss Priss, and the weeks were mounting up. Her return had receded into a vague worry which was becoming vaguer every day.

She was in the consulting rooms in good time on Monday morning, for although the doctor might not be there there was plenty to do. She sorted the post and laid it ready on his desk, noting with a small sigh of relief that there was no envelope with Miss Priss's spiky writing on it.

That letter was in the doctor's pocket, for it had been sent to his house. He had read it and then read it again; Miss Priss's mother had died and she would be glad to return to work as soon as she had settled her affairs.

I shall give up our home. It is a rented house and I do not wish to remain here. Would you consider allowing me to live in the flat on the top floor of the consulting rooms? I would be happy to receive a reduced salary in this case, or pay rent. I have no family and few friends here and must find somewhere to live. I would not have suggested this, but I have worked for you for so many years that I feel I can venture to give voice to this possible arrangement.

Of course he would agree to it; Miss Priss was a trusted right hand, had been for years, and the arrangement would give her a secure future and a home. She must be in her fifties, he thought, at a time in life when the years ahead should offer that security. A letter, reassuring her, must be written, and Loveday must be told.

The answer to Loveday, as far as he was concerned, was to marry her. But first he must allow her to get over Charles and, that done, he would wait until the cracks in her heart were healed. But in the meantime she would need a roof over her head...

He wrote reassuringly to Miss Priss: she was to have the flat and to resume her duties just as soon as she felt able. He suggested two weeks ahead. He would be delighted to have her back and she was to regard the flat as her home until such time as she might wish to leave.

The letter written, he turned his thoughts to Loveday. Before he told her, he decided, he would drive down to the remote village where her aunt lived.

The orderly days slid by and it seemed to him that Loveday was beginning to forget Charles. She was quiet, but then she always was; however, her face in repose was no longer sad.

Early on Saturday morning he started on the long drive to the village on Dartmoor with Bob propped up beside him. It would probably be a wild-goose chase but it was the obvious thing to do...

It was a journey of about two hundred miles, but once free of London and its sprawling suburbs the road was fairly empty, and the further west he went the emptier it became. On a quiet stretch of road he stopped for coffee and to see to Bob's needs, and then he drove on until he reached the bypass to Exeter and took the road to the moor. Presently he turned off and drove through Ashburton and into the empty country beyond. It was a clear late-autumn day and the majestic sweep of the moorland hills swept away from him into the distance. The road was narrow now, and sheep roamed to and fro between the craggy rocks. Bob, who had never seen a sheep, was entranced.

The village, when he reached it, was charming, built on the banks of the river Dart and surrounded by trees. It had a handful of grey stone houses and an ancient church, a cheerful-looking pub and one or two bigger houses near the church. The doctor stopped at the pub and went inside.

The bar was small and cosy, with a bright log fire burning and comfortable chairs set beside the tables. It would be a focal point in the village, he reflected, and a cheerful haven on a bleak winter's evening.

Of course he could have lunch, said the elderly man behind the bar. A pasty and a pint of the best ale in the country, and the dog was welcome to come in.

Bob, carried in and sat gently on the floor, caused quite a stir. The two young men playing darts abandoned their game to come and look at his plastered legs and an old man by the fire declared that he'd never seen anything like it before. Their interest in him engendered a friendly atmosphere and a still deeper interest when the doctor mentioned that he had driven down from London.

'Lost, are you?' one of the young men wanted to know.

'No, no. I've come to visit someone living here. A Miss West?'

'Up at Bates Cottage?' volunteered the landlord, setting down the pasty and a bowl of water for Bob. 'Know her, do you, sir? Elderly, like, and not given to visitors?'

He looked at the doctor with frank curiosity.

'I have never met her. I have come to see her on behalf of her niece.'

'Oh, aye, she's got a niece—sends her a card at Christmas. Me ma cleans for her and sees to her post and shopping. She told Miss West she should have her niece to stay, but the old lady's independent, like, don't want to be a nuisance.'

'I should like to go and see her this afternoon...'

'As good a time as any. It's the last house at the end of the lane past the church. Too big for her, but she won't move. Got her dogs and cats and birds.'

'Could you put me up for the night?' asked the doctor.

'That I can,' said the landlord. 'And you could do with a nice bit of supper, no doubt?'

'Indeed I could. I'll go and call on Miss West before it gets dark.' He paid his bill, ordered pints all round, picked up Bob and went back to the car. It was no distance to Miss West's house, but unless she invited Bob in he would have to stay in the car.

The house was built of grey stone and thatched, and it was a good deal larger than the other cottages in the village. The curtains were undrawn and in the beginnings of an early dusk the lamplight from the room beside the stout front door shone cheerfully.

He went up the path and tugged the old-fashioned bell.

The elderly lady who opened it was small and brisk.

'I'm Miss West. Are you looking for me? If so why? I don't know you.'

The doctor perceived that he would need his bedside manner.

'I apologise for calling upon you in this manner, but first I must ask you if you are indeed the aunt of Loveday West?'

She stood staring at him. 'Yes, I am. Come inside.' She peered past him. 'What is that in your car?'

'My dog.'

'Fetch him.'

'He has two legs in plaster and is somewhat of an invalid.'

'All the more reason to bring him inside.'

When he'd fetched Bob she led the way from the narrow hall to the sitting room, which was nicely lighted, warmed by a brisk open fire and comfortably furnished.

'While you are explaining why you have come to see me we may as well have tea. Sit there, near the fire— your dog can sit on the rug.'

The doctor did as he was told. 'His name is Bob.'

Now that he was in the lighted room he could see her clearly. She was in her late sixties or early seventies, he judged, and what she lacked in height she made up for by the strength of her personality. A lady to be reckoned with, he reflected, feeling a little amused, with her plain face, fierce dark eyes and iron-grey hair tugged back into an old-fashioned bun at the back of her head.

He sat down with Bob's head on his feet. He had liked the old lady on sight, but wondered if he was making a mistake. He would know that when he had told her about Loveday.

He got up and took the tea tray from her as she came back into the room. He set it on a small table, then waited until she had sat down before resuming his seat. Good manners came to him as naturally as breathing. Miss West, pouring the tea, liked him for that.

'If I might introduce myself?' suggested the doctor, accepting a cup of tea. 'Andrew Fforde—I'm a doctor. I have a practice in London and work at a London hospital.'

Miss West, sitting very upright in her chair, nodded. 'Give Bob a biscuit. Is he good with cats?'

'My housekeeper has a cat; they get on well together.'

'Then be good enough to open the kitchen door so that my cats and Tim can come in.'

He did as he was asked and three cats came into the sitting room. None of them in their first youth, they ignored Bob and sat down in a tidy row before the fire. Plodding along behind them was an odd dog, with a grey muzzle and a friendly eye, who breathed over Bob and sat down heavily on the doctor's feet.

Miss West passed him the cake dish. 'I have not seen Loveday since she was a very small girl. She wrote to me when her other aunt died. She made it plain that she was living in easy circumstances and has never asked for help of any kind. We exchange cards at Christmas. I have thought of her as one of these young women with a career and a wish to live their own lives without encumbrances of any sort.' She sipped her tea from a delicate china cup. 'Perhaps I have been mistaken?'

When he didn't answer, she said, 'Tell me what you have come to tell me.'

He put down his cup and saucer and told her. He added no embellishments and no opinions of his own, and when he had finished he added, 'It seemed to me right that you should know this…'

'Is she pretty?'

'No, I think perhaps one would call her rather plain. But she has a beauty which has nothing to do with looks. She has beautiful green eyes and soft mousy hair. She is small and she has a charming voice.'

'Fat? Thin?'

'Slim and nicely rounded.'

'You're in love with her?'

'Yes. I hope to marry her, but first she must recover from her meeting with Charles.'

Miss West stroked a cat which had climbed onto her lap. 'How old are you?'

'Thirty-eight. Loveday is twenty-four.'

'I like you, Dr Fforde. I don't like many people, and I have only just met you, nevertheless, I like you. Do whatever you think is the best for Loveday, and bring her here until she is ready to go with you as your wife.'

'That will be for her to decide,' he said quietly. 'But if she chooses to go her own way, then I shall make sure that she has a good job and a secure future.'

Miss West said, 'You love her as much as that?'

'Yes.' He smiled at her. 'Thank you for seeing me and giving me your willing help. May I let you know if our plans will be possible? It depends upon Loveday.'

'If Loveday decides to come and stay with me I shall make her welcome. And I wish you luck, Dr Fforde.'

'Thank you.' He would need it, he reflected on his way back to the pub. He had no right to interfere in Loveday's life and she would probably tell him so…

The small bar was full, and although he was stared at with frank curiosity, they were friendly stares.

The landlord, drawing him a pint, asked cheerfully if he had found Miss West. 'Nice old lady—lived here for a lifetime, she has. Don't hold with travel. There's a steak pie and our own sprouts for your supper, sir. Seven o'clock suit you? And if you let me know what your dog will eat…?' He eyed Bob, braced against the doctor's legs. 'Nice little beast. Seeing as he's an invalid, like, I'll put an old rug in your room for him.'

The doctor slept soundly. He had done what he had come to do, though whether it was the right thing only time would tell.

As for Bob, he was with his master and that was all that mattered to him. He had had a splendid supper and the old rug was reassuringly rich in smells: of wood ash and spilt food and ingrained dirt from boots. Just the thing to soothe a dog to sleep.

The doctor left after an unhurried breakfast, taking his time over the return trip to London. He had a lot to think about and he could do that undisturbed. He stopped for coffee and to accommodate Bob's needs and then, since the road was almost empty, he didn't stop again until he reached home.

Mrs Duckett spent Sunday afternoons with her sister and the house was quiet. But there was soup keeping warm on the Aga and cold meat and salad set out on the kitchen table. There was a note from Mrs Duckett telling him that she would cook him his dinner when she returned later.

He fed Bob and went to his study, to immerse himself in work. There was always plenty of paper-work; even with the secretary who came twice a week his desk was never empty. It wasn't until a faint aroma of something delicious caused him to twitch his splendid nose that he paused. Mrs Duckett was back and he was hungry.

Loveday went to bed early in her little flat, happily unaware of the future which was to be so soon disturbed.

The next day the doctor was due to go to the hospital after he had seen his patients at the consulting rooms, and he would be there for the rest of the day, but there was almost half an hour before he needed to leave. He went into the waiting room and found Loveday filing away patients' notes and writing up his daily diary ready for the morning.

She looked up as he went in. 'I'll type those two letters and leave them on your desk,' she told him. 'If there's anything urgent I could phone you at the hospital?'

'Yes, I'm booked up for the morning, aren't I? Use your discretion and fit in patients where you can. Anything really urgent, refer them to me at the hospital. I shall be there until six o'clock at least.'

He leaned against the desk, looking at her. 'I had a letter from Miss Priss. Her mother has died and she asks to come back to work in ten days' time; she also asks if she might have the flat in which to live. She has no family and her mother's house was rented.'

Loveday had gone a little pale. 'I'm so sorry Miss Priss's mother has died. But I'm glad that she has somewhere to come to where she can make her home. When would you like me to leave?'

'In a week's time? That gives me ample opportunity to ask around and find another similar job for you. I know a great many people and it shouldn't be too difficult.'

She said quickly, 'That is very kind of you, but I'm sure that I can find work...'

He said harshly, 'You will allow me to help you? I have no intention of allowing you to be homeless and workless. You came here to fill an emergency at my request; you will at least allow me to pay my debt.'

'Isn't a week rather a short time? I mean to find another job for me? Besides, you're busy all day...'

It was just the opening he had hoped for. 'Perhaps it may take longer than a week. You told me that you have an aunt living in Devon. Would you go and stay with her until I can get you fixed up?'

'But I've never seen her, at least not since I was a very little girl, and she might not want to have me to stay. And it's miles away...'

He said quietly, 'I went to see your aunt on Saturday, after I received Miss Priss's letter. You see, Loveday, I had to think of something quickly. She is quite elderly and I liked her—and she is both eager and willing for you to stay with her until you can get settled again.'

'You went all that way to see my aunt? Your weekend wasted...?'

'Not wasted, and, as I said, I like to pay my debts, Loveday.'

He straightened up and went to the door. 'Will you think about it and let me know in the morning? It's a sensible solution to the problem, you know.'

He smiled at her then, and went away. He wanted very much to stay and comfort her, to tell her that she had no need to worry, that he would look after her and love her. Instead he had told her everything in a matter-of-fact voice which gave away none of his feelings. The temptation to cajole her into accepting his offer was great, but he resisted it. He wanted her to love him—but only of her own free will.

Loveday sat very still; she felt as though someone had hit her very hard on the head and taken away her power to think. She had managed to answer the doctor sensibly, matching his own matter-of-fact manner, but now there was no need to do that. A week, she thought—seven days in which to find a job. She would have to start finding it at once, for of course there was no question of her accepting his offer of help.

She began to cry quietly. Not because she was once more with an undecided future but because that future would be without him. This calm, quiet man who had come to her rescue and who, she had no doubt, once he had made sure that she had another job, would dismiss her from his mind. She gave a great sniff, wiping the tears away with the back of her hand. After all, he had Mrs Seward, hadn't he?

Loveday, who had never felt jealous in her life before, was suddenly flooded with it.

Presently she stopped crying; it was a waste of time and was of no help at all. She put away the rest of the patients' notes, and then, since she would have the afternoon to get things ready for the next day, she selected the most likely newspapers and magazines to contain job advertisements and took herself off to the flat.

She explained it all to Sam, who yawned and went back to sleep, so she made a pot of tea, cut a sandwich and sat down to look through the job vacancy columns. There were plenty of vacancies—all of them for those with computer skills or, failing that, willing to undertake kitchen duties or work in launderettes. Since she had no knowledge of computers it would have to be something domestic. And why stay in London? Since she wouldn't see the doctor again, the further away she got from him the better.

'Out of sight, out of mind,' said Loveday, and because she was unhappy, and a little afraid of the future, she started to cry again.

But not for long. Presently she restored her face to its normal, or almost normal appearance and went back to the consulting room. She tidied up and got everything ready for the next day, made several appointments too, and brought the daily diary up to date, and when Mrs Seward phoned during the afternoon she answered her in a pleasant manner.

It was hard to dislike Mrs Seward; she was friendly and she had a nice voice. She sighed when Loveday told her that the doctor was at the hospital.

'I'll ring there and see if I can leave a message,' she told Loveday, 'but leave a note on his desk, will you? It's not urgent, but I do want to talk to him.'

Loveday went to bed early, since sitting alone in the flat while her thoughts tumbled around in her head was of no use, but her last waking thought was that nothing would persuade her to accept the doctor's suggestion.

When she sorted out the post in the morning there was a letter for her. From her aunt.

It was a long letter, written in a spidery hand, and, typically of Miss West, didn't beat about the bush. She had had a visit from Dr Fforde and agreed with him that the sensible thing to do was for Loveday to spend a few days with her while suitable work was found for her.

> *It is obvious that he is a man who has influence and moreover feels that he is indebted to you, as indeed he is. We know nothing of each other, but I shall be glad of your company. We are, after all, family. I live very quietly, but from what I hear from Dr Fforde you are not one of these modern career girls. I look forward to seeing you.*

There was a PS: *Bring your cat with you.*

Dr Fforde, wishing her good morning later on that day, noted that she had been crying, but her ordinary face, rather pink in the nose and puffed around the eyes, was composed.

'I have had a letter from my aunt, explaining that you have been to see her and inviting me to stay until I've another job.'

And when he didn't answer, but stood quietly, watching her, she said, 'I expect it would be more convenient to you if I go and stay with her. So may I leave on Saturday? I expect Miss Priss would like to come as soon as it can be arranged.' She gave him a brave smile which tore at his heart. 'If I go early on Saturday morning she could have the weekend to move in. I'll leave everything ready for her.'

'That sounds admirable. I will drive you down to your aunt on Saturday morning.'

She said quickly, 'No, no. There's no need. I haven't much luggage and I'm sure there is a splendid train service.'

'None the less I will drive you and Sam, Loveday.'

She knew better than to argue when he spoke in that quiet voice.

'Well, thank you. And if you will write and let me know if you hear of a job?' She added hastily, 'Oh, I'm sure you will, because you said so, but I could always go to Exeter. There is sure to be something there…'

She looked very young standing there, and he was so much older. He was sure she probably thought of him as middle-aged. He said gently, 'If you would trust me, Loveday…'

'Oh, I do. You must know that.'

He smiled then, and went to his consulting room.

Loveday and he would be leaving, she told Sam, and she bought a cat basket which he viewed with suspicion. He was suspicious too when she started to spring-clean the flat. The little place must be left pristine, she told herself.

It kept her busy when she wasn't at work, so that she was tired enough to sleep for at least part of the night, but waking in the early hours of the morning there was nothing else to do but go over and over her problems.

The greatest of these, she quickly discovered, was how she was going to live without seeing the doctor each day. She supposed that she hadn't thought much about it before; he was always there, each day, and she had accepted that, not looking ahead. Even when she had supposed her heart to be broken by Charles there had always been the thought that the doctor was there, quiet in the background of her muddled mind.

He had become part of her life without her realising it and now there was nothing to be done about it. Falling

in love, she discovered, wasn't anything like the in-
fatuation she had had for Charles. It was the slow
awareness of knowing that you wanted to be with
someone for the rest of your life…

The days passed too quickly. She packed her small
possessions, scoured the flat once more, said goodbye
to Todd, and left the waiting room in a state of perfec-
tion and the filing cabinet in perfect order.

At the doctor's quiet request she presented herself
with her case and Sam in his basket sharp on Saturday
morning at nine o'clock. Somehow the leaving was
made easier by the fact that he had told her to leave
anything she wouldn't need at her aunt's, in the attic
next to the flat. It seemed to her a kind of crack in the
door, as it were.

With Sam grumbling in his basket on the back seat
and Bob beside him, they set off. The doctor had bidden
her a cheerful good morning, observing that it should
be a pleasant trip.

'I have always liked the late autumn,' he told her,
'even though the days are short. You've brought warm
clothing with you? Miss West has a charming house,
and the village is just as charming, but it is rather
remote—though I believe there's a bus service to
Ashburton once a week.' He glanced sideways at her
small profile and added cheerfully, 'Probably you
won't be there long enough to try it out.'

'You haven't heard of anything that I could do?' she
asked, then added quickly, 'I'm sorry. There was no
need for me to say that. How can you have had the
time? I thought that if there is nothing after a week or
ten days I could go into Exeter and look around for a
job there.'

'A good idea,' said the doctor, not meaning a word of it. He knew exactly what he was going to do.

They stopped for coffee at a small wayside café on the A303, and Bob, his legs out of plaster now, went for a careful walk. Sam in his basket, somnolent after a big breakfast, hardly stirred.

It was impossible to feel unhappy; the man she had discovered that she loved was here beside her. Perhaps after today she might not see him again, but just for the moment she was happy. They didn't talk much, but when they did it was to discover that they liked the same things—the country, books, animals, winter evenings by the fire, walking in the moonlight. Oh, I do hope Mrs Seward likes the same things, thought Loveday. I want him to be happy.

They stopped for lunch at a hotel a few miles short of Exeter and then went on their way again—on the Plymouth road now, until they reached Ashburton and turned away from the main road and presently reached the village.

Miss West had the door open before the doctor had stopped the car in front of it. He got out, opened Loveday's door and tucked her hand in his.

'Your niece Loveday, Miss West,' he said.

CHAPTER FIVE

LOVEDAY had grown more and more silent the nearer they had got to Buckland-in-the Moor. It had been a grey overcast day, and once they had left Ashburton behind the moor had stretched before them, magnificent and remote. She had had the nasty feeling that she shouldn't have come; her aunt might not like her, the doctor might not be able to find her another job and, worst of all, she might never see him again.

The lane they'd been driving along had taken a sharp bend and there before them had been the village, tucked beside the river Dart, and as though there had been a prearranged signal a beam of watery sunshine had escaped from the cloud.

'It's beautiful,' Loveday had said, and had suddenly felt much better. She'd turned to look at the doctor.

'I knew you would like it, Loveday,' he had said quietly, but he hadn't looked as he'd driven into the cluster of cottages, past the church, and stopped at Miss West's house.

She'd said in sudden panic, 'You won't go…?'

'No, I shall spend the night at the pub and drive back tomorrow.'

She had let out a small sigh of relief and got out when he'd opened her door, then stood for a moment looking at her aunt's home. There was no front garden, only a grass verge, and at this time of year the grey stone walls looked bleak and unwelcoming, but she had forgotten that when the door had opened and her aunt had stood there with a welcome warm enough to cheer the faintest heart.

Now in the narrow hall, she stopped to study Loveday. 'Your mother had green eyes,' she observed. 'I'm glad that we shall have the chance to get to know each other. You may call me Aunt Leticia.'

She turned to the doctor. 'You had a good journey?' She looked past him. 'The cat and your dog? They are in the car?'

'A very pleasant drive. Bob and Sam are in the car.'

'Good. There is a conservatory leading from the kitchen; Sam may go there for the moment. There is food—everything that he may need. Bob may come into the sitting room.'

She was urging Loveday before her and said over her shoulder, 'Her cases can wait; we will have tea. Take your coats off.'

Loveday did as she was told, and the doctor, amused, did the same, with a nostalgic memory of a fierce, much loved nanny speaking to him in just such a voice.

They had tea, a proper tea, sitting at a round table under the windows while the dogs and cats lay in a companionable heap before the fire. Presently a cautious Sam crept in and joined them, and since none of the animals did more than open an eye he settled down with all the appearance of someone who had come home...

The doctor fetched the cases presently and took his leave, but not before Aunt Leticia had bidden him to Sunday lunch.

'I attend Matins on Sunday mornings,' she told him, 'but I'm sure that you and Loveday will wish to discuss her future. A good walk in the fresh air will do you both good. Fetch her at ten o'clock. You can walk across to Holne and have coffee there. Lunch will be at one o'clock and then she and I will go to Evensong.'

The doctor, recognising an ally, agreed meekly, thanked the old lady for his tea, said a cheerful good-night to Loveday and took himself and Bob off to the pub, where he was welcomed like an old friend. And later, after a good supper and a quick walk with Bob, he went to bed and slept the sleep of a man untroubled by his future.

Loveday, having repressed a strong desire to run out of the house after him, followed her aunt upstairs to a little room overlooking the back garden and the moor beyond. It was austerely furnished, and had the look of not having had an occupant for a long time, but there were books on the bedside table and a vase of chrysanthemums on the old-fashioned dressing table, and when she was left to unpack her things and opened the wardrobe and stiff drawers there was the delightful scent of lavender.

She went downstairs presently and helped to feed the cats and Tim, surprised to find that Sam seemed quite at home.

'I have always found animals better friends than people,' said Aunt Leticia, 'and they know that. When you go into the garden take care; there is a family of hedgehogs in the compost heap and rabbits in the hedge.'

They spent a pleasant evening together, looking at old photos of family Loveday scarcely remembered, and then, over their supper, Miss West began asking careful questions.

Loveday, enjoying the luxury of having someone to talk to, told her about Miss Cattell and then the doctor. Talking about him made him seem nearer, and her aunt, looking at her niece's ordinary face, saw how it lighted up when she talked of him.

Well, reflected Miss West, Loveday was an ice child. No looks worth mentioning, but with eyes like that looks didn't matter. The doctor was a good deal older, of course, but she didn't think that would matter in the least. He was clearly in love and suspected that Loveday was too, but for some reason she was denying it, even to herself. Ah, well, thought Miss West wisely, all that's needed is a little patience—and absence makes the heart grow fonder...

Loveday, with Sam for company, slept dreamlessly. Her last thoughts had been of the doctor and were the first on waking too. He would go away today, but there was the morning first...

She got up, dressed and went downstairs. She helped get the breakfast and saw to the animals and her aunt, who had liked her on sight, found the liking turning to affection. Loveday was a sensible girl who made no fuss and helped around the house without making a song and dance about it. She'll make Dr Fforde a good wife, reflected Aunt Leticia.

The doctor knocked on the door at ten o'clock, and after a few minutes chatting with Miss West he marched

Loveday off at a brisk pace. Bob had come with him but he had already had a walk and now he was sitting contentedly in the sitting room with Tim. As the doctor explained, a long walk would be too tiring for his weak legs.

'Holne is about a mile away,' he told Loveday as they took the narrow road past the church. 'I'm told that we can get coffee there at the pub. Then we can follow the river towards Widecombe. There's a path.'

He began to talk about everything and nothing, with not a word about the future, and because she was so happy with him she forgot for the moment that she had no future and chatted away about the dogs and cats and the hedgehogs in the garden.

'I do like my aunt,' she told him. 'It must be difficult for her to have me living with her, even for a few days; she's lived alone for a long time and she told me that she was happy to be on her own. I expect she knows everyone in the village—she doesn't seem lonely.'

'I'm sure she will enjoy your company. Here's Holne and the pub—shall we stop for coffee?'

The coffee was excellent and there was a great log fire in the bar, but they didn't stay too long. They took the path close to the river and now it was the doctor's turn to tell her about his own life. Oh, yes, he told her when she asked, he had a mother, living in Lincolnshire where his father had had a practice before he died. 'And sisters,' he went on. 'You have met Margaret at the consulting room.'

Loveday came to a halt. 'I thought that she—that you—well, I thought you were going to marry her.'

She went red, although she looked him in the face.

He didn't allow himself to smile. So that was why she had pokered up… Another obstacle out of the way, he reflected. First Charles and now this. The temptation to take her in his arms there and then was great, but there was one more obstacle—the difference in their ages. He must give her time to think about that…

He said lightly, 'I've always been too busy to get married.' They were walking on now. 'And you, Loveday, have you no wish to marry?'

'Yes, but only to the right man.' She didn't want to talk about that. 'Do you suppose we should be turning back?'

He accepted her change in the conversation without comment.

They walked back the way they had come and the chilly bright morning began to cloud over. When they were within sight of the cottage, Loveday said, 'You will let me know…? I'm sorry to keep reminding you, but I'd like to be certain.'

'I promise you that I will let you know, and now that we are no longer working together could you not call me Andrew?'

She smiled suddenly. 'I've always called you Andrew inside my head,' she told him.

Lunch was a cheerful meal. Aunt Leticia might live alone, but she was aware of all that went on in the world so far removed from her home. There was plenty to talk about—until she said reluctantly, 'You will want to be on your way, and I mustn't keep you. Loveday, get your coat and walk up to the pub and see Dr Fforde safely away.'

The walk was short—far too short. Only a matter of a couple of minutes. Loveday stood by the car while the doctor invited Bob onto the back seat, closed the car door and turned to her.

He took her hands in his and stood looking down at her. The scarf she had tied over her mousy locks had done nothing to enhance her appearance. She looked about sixteen years old, and the last obstacle, the difference in their ages, was suddenly very real. He would marry her, but not until she had had the chance to lead her own life to meet people—young men—who would make her laugh as Charles had done.

All the things he wanted to say were unsaid. He wished her goodbye and got into the car and drove away.

She watched it through tear-filled eyes until it disappeared round the curve in the lane. Just for a moment she had thought that he was going to say something— that he would see her again, that they would keep in touch, remain friends…

She wiped her eyes and went back to Aunt Leticia. She helped with the washing up and then took the elderly Tim for his ambling walk, and later went to Evensong with her aunt. No one, looking at her quiet face, would have guessed how unhappy she was.

The days which followed were quiet, centred round the simple life Aunt Leticia lived, but there was always something to do. She often walked to Holne, a mile away, where there was a Post Office, and to the nearby farm for eggs, and halfway through each week she was sent to Ashburton on the weekly bus, armed with a shopping list—groceries and meat, wool for her aunt's knitting, and food for the cats and Tim. There was the weekly excitement of the travelling library, and the daily collecting of the newspapers from the pub.

The landlord liked a good gossip in his slow friendly voice; he was too kind a man to ask questions, but life in the village was quiet and her arrival had made a nice little break now that there were no visitors passing through. He had taken to the doctor, too, and had several times confided in his wife that there was more to his visits than met the eye...

It was late on a Saturday evening by the time the doctor arrived at the pub. It was too late to call on Miss West, so it was early on Sunday morning when Loveday got up to let Tim and the cats out and saw him coming down the lane.

She ran to the door and flung it wide as he reached it, and went into his arms with the unselfconsciousness of a child.

He closed the door gently behind them and then wrapped his arms around her again.

'I had to come. I had to know. You see, my darling Loveday, I'm in love with you...'

'Then why didn't you say so?' she asked fiercely.

'I'm so much older than you, and you have never had the chance to meet men of your own age. Only Charles.'

She dismissed Charles with a sniff. 'Is that your only reason?' She hesitated. 'I'm dull and plain and not at all clever. I'd be a very unexciting wife for someone like you.'

'I find you very exciting,' he told her, and kissed her, and presently said, 'You shall have all the time in the world to decide if you will marry me. I'll go back to London this evening and not come again until you can give me an answer.'

She looked at him then, and said in a shaky little voice, 'I'll stay here as long as you want me to, but I'll give you my answer now. I love you too, and I'll marry you—today if we could.'

He looked down at her earnest, loving face and smiled. Fourteen years were nothing; they simply didn't matter. He kissed her again, very thoroughly—a delightful experience which, naturally enough, was repeated.

Aunt Leticia, coming downstairs to put the kettle on made no effort to disturb them. Putting tea leaves into the teapot, she reflected that she would give them the silver pot which had belonged to her great-great-grandmother for a wedding present. She took her tea and sat by the Aga, waiting patiently. Let them have their lovely moment.